The Unofficial Official Handbook for Boys

The Unofficial Official Handbook for Boys

LONDON, NEW YORK, MUNICH,
MELBOURNE, DELHI

Text written by L.L. Buller

Project Art Editor Lee Riches

Editorial Lead Heather Jones

DTP Designers
David McDonald, Nicoline Thilert

Special Sales Production Manager
Silvia La Greca

Associate Publisher Nigel Duffield

Boy Scouts of America

The mission of the Boys Scouts of America is to prepare young people to make ethical and moral choices over their lifetimes by instilling in them the values of the Scout Oath and Law. The programs of the Boy Scouts of America—Cub Scouting, Boy Scouting, Varsity Scouting, and Venturing— pursue these aims through methods designed for the age and maturity of the participants.

Cub Scouting: A family- and home-centered program for boys in the first through fifth grade (or 7, 8, 9, and 10 years old). Cub Scouting's emphasis is on quality programs at the local level, where the most boys and families are involved. Fourth- and fifth-grade (or 10-year-old) boys are called Webelos (WE'll BE LOyal Scouts) and participate in more advanced activities that begin to prepare them to become

Boy Scouts.

Boy Scouting: A program for boys 11 through 17 designed to acheive the aims of Scouting through a vigorous outdoor program and peer group leadership with the counsel of an adult Scoutmaster. (Boys may also become Boy Scouts if they have earned the Arrow of Light Award or have completed the fifth grade.)

Varsity Scouting: An active, exciting program for young men 14 through 17 built around five program fields of emphasis: advancement, high adventure, personal development, service, and special programs, and events.

Venturing: This is for young men and young women ages 14 through 20. It includes challenging high-adventure activities, sports, and hobbies for teenagers that teach leadership skills, provide opportunities to teach others, and to learn and grow in a supporting, caring, and fun environment.

For more information about Boy Scouts of America or its programs visit www.scouting.org

http://www.scouting.org

First American Edition, 2008

Published in the United States by DK Publishing, Inc. 375 Hudson Street,
New York, New York 10014

07 08 09 10 11 10 9 8 7 6 5 4 3 2 1

Copyright © 2008 Dorling Kindersley Limited

www.scouting.org

A Cataloging-in-Publication record for this book is available from the Library of Congress.

ISBN 978-0756-638054

DK books are available at special discounts for bulk purchases for sales promotions, premiums, fund-raising, or educational use. For details, contact: DK Publishing Special Markets, 375 Hudson Street, New York, NY 10014 or SpecialSales@dk.com

Color reproduction by GRB, Italy

Printed and bound in China by L.REX Printing Company.

Discover more at
www.dk.com

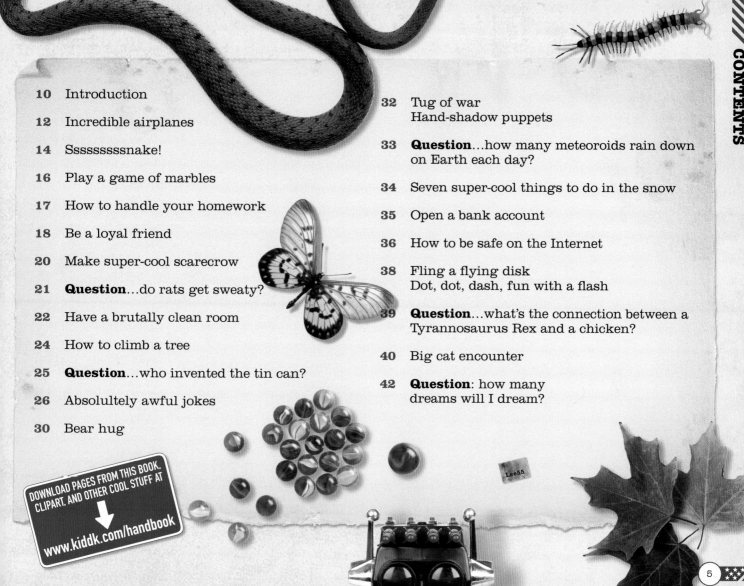

10   Introduction

12   Incredible airplanes

14   Sssssssssnake!

16   Play a game of marbles

17   How to handle your homework

18   Be a loyal friend

20   Make super-cool scarecrow

21   **Question**…do rats get sweaty?

22   Have a brutally clean room

24   How to climb a tree

25   **Question**…who invented the tin can?

26   Absolultely awful jokes

30   Bear hug

32   Tug of war
        Hand-shadow puppets

33   **Question**…how many meteoroids rain down on Earth each day?

34   Seven super-cool things to do in the snow

35   Open a bank account

36   How to be safe on the Internet

38   Fling a flying disk
        Dot, dot, dash, fun with a flash

39   **Question**…what's the connection between a Tyrannosaurus Rex and a chicken?

40   Big cat encounter

42   **Question**: how many dreams will I dream?

Lee55

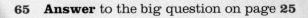

43 Hostage!
Adopt a tree

44 My notes

46 Ornithology

48 My notes: keeping track

50 Be safe, wherever you are

52 My safety notes

54 Make the most soak-tastic water balloons ever
Let me twist your arm

55 **Answer**…how many meteoroids rain down on Earth each day?

56 Make your own sidewalk chalk

57 Answer to the big question on page **39**!

58 Set up a tantalizing treasure hunt

60 Amazing arthropods

62 Collect fireflies

64 Snowball fight!

65 **Answer** to the big question on page **25**

66 Write your town's biography

68 Herpetology

70 Fix a yummy after-school snack

72 Answer to the big question on page **21**

73 Recycle your old jeans into a cool book bag

74 **Question**…how many words can you write with just one pencil?

75 Manhunt!
Gotcha

76 Hold a soap-bubble blowing contest

78 Run the best lemonade stand in the entire world

79 The way to wash your wheels (and the rest of your bike)

80 Ichthyology

82 Give the planet a hug

84 Everything there possibly could be to know about recycling

86 Make sure your stuff is unbearable (for bears)

88 Be nice to your sister
   Hang up a hammock, climb in, and relaxxxxxx

89 Super slime

90 Make a worm farm

92 Astounding tricks to confound your friends

94 **Question**...where did spaghetti come from anyway?

95 Volunteer!

96 Amazing animal facts

98 Alligator encounter

100 Track animals by their scats

102 The most twisted tongue-twisters ever collected

104 Who sees seashells by the seashore?

106 Cool tricks to do with a jump rope

107 Rake a big pile of leaves and jump in

108 **Question**: could you really fry an egg on the sidewalk on a hot day?

109 Whittle a walking stick

109 Banish a bug from your house

110 Take a hike!

112 Alien encounter

114 Avalanche!

116 Do a good deed today

117 **Question**: do frogs have ears?

118 Shark attack

120 How to catch a snake

121 **Answer** to the big question on page 42

122 Crystals

124 Say hello to the world!

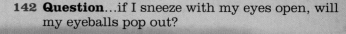

CONTENTS

125 **Answer** to the big question on page **94**

126 Skeleton

128 Entomology

130 Fun things to do with your family

132 How tall is that tree?

134 Make a bird buffet

135 **Answer** to the big question on page **74**

136 A dozen dandy things to do with a bandanna

137 Leave no trace

138 Get your head in the clouds

140 **Question**…if I do my homework every night, will my brain get bigger?

141 How to build an amazing campfire

142 **Question**…if I sneeze with my eyes open, will my eyeballs pop out?

143 Make brilliant bug traps!

144 Pack it up! All the stuff you need for camping

146 Gimmie grub

148 Gimmie a break

149 **Answer** to the big question on page **117**

150 Ten things to do in a tent when it's raining cats and dogs outside

152 What's the best pet to get?

154 **Answer** to the big question on page **142**

155 How to blow a blade of grass
Paper, rock, scissors

156 Hot diggety dogs

157 S'mores galore

BE SAFE, WHEREVER YOU ARE

158 What is the world's largest flower?

159 Way-cool willow wigwam

160 **Question**...are there really robots on Mars?

161 Incredible numbers

162 The best paper airplane to ever fly the sky

163 Fold an origami swan
Hats off to you!

164 Cover your room in spider webs
How to juggle three beanbags

165 **Answer** to the big question on page 108

166 How to steal home plate

167 **Answer** to the big question on page 158

168 Ten strange and fascinating facts about
everybody's body (including yours)

170 Superlative sit-ups and powerful push-ups

172 Escape from a swarm of bees

174 How to shoot a slap shot

175 **Answer** to the big question on page 140

176 How to slam-dunk a basketball

177 How to catch a Hail Mary pass

178 Ten mind-boggling transportation facts

180 How to score a penalty kick

181 **Answer** to the big question on page 160

182 Show your respect for the stars and stripes

184 Tag You're it.
How to avoid itchy, scratchy poisonous plants

186 The end

187 Index

HEY, YOU!
YES, YOU.
OPEN ME UP AND TAKE A LOOK.

I KNOW WHAT YOU'RE THINKING... IS THIS BOOK REALLY TALKING TO ME?

YES, I AM. SO LISTEN UP: There is no official handbook for being a kid. You didn't exactly come with directions. But if you want to learn stuff, and do stuff, and experience stuff, all the instructions you need are right between the covers of this book.

Think of it as a **secret guidebook** for cool kid stuff. It's a little bit random, but then life's like that. It's a little bit out there, but when was that ever a bad thing? It's a lot of fun, but that's OK with you, right? There's tons of **information**, **facts**, and **trivia** to fill up your brain. You'll also find plenty of **activities**, **games**, and things to do to jump-start your body. Because after all, being a kid is fun. **Go on, take a look**.

You're going to find something good. I'll bet you'll find something surprising, too. (And I hope there's lots of stuff in here that you don't already know.) It's officially official:

THIS BOOK IS MADE JUST FOR YOU.

Passenger Jet

De Havilland Comet

Lockheed Electra

Concorde

P-51 D Mustang

Jumbo Jet

Red Arrows

Spitfire

Republic P-47
Thunderbolt

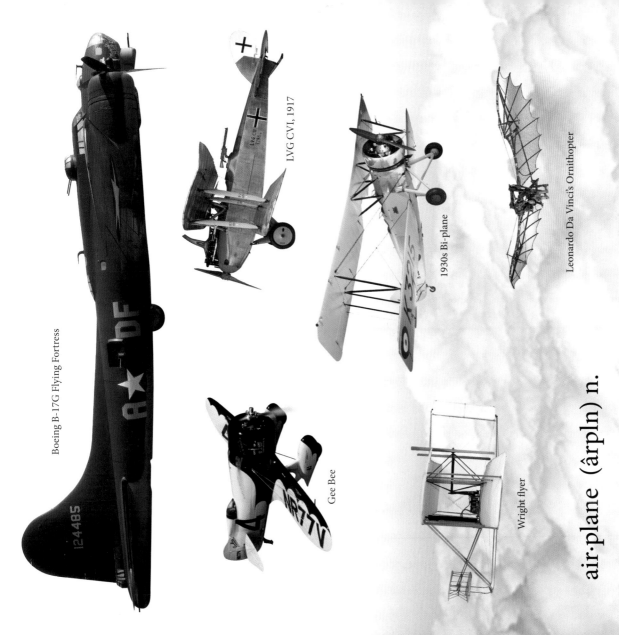

Boeing B-17G Flying Fortress

LVG CVI, 1917

1930s Bi-plane

Leonardo Da Vinci's Ornithopter

Gee Bee

Wright flyer

air·plane (ârpln) n.

Any of various winged vehicles capable of
flight, generally heavier than air and driven
by jet engines or propellers.

SSSSSS

DOES THE IDEA OF STUMBLING ACROSS A SNAKE LEAVE YOUR INSIDES COILED IN FEAR?

There's no need to be **hysssssssterical**. When hiking or camping in snake country, keep these tips in mind, and you'll slither out of any trouble. Most importantly, make sure that someone in your group carries a snakebite kit, and knows how to use it. You don't want to go down in **hissssstory** for the wrong reasons!

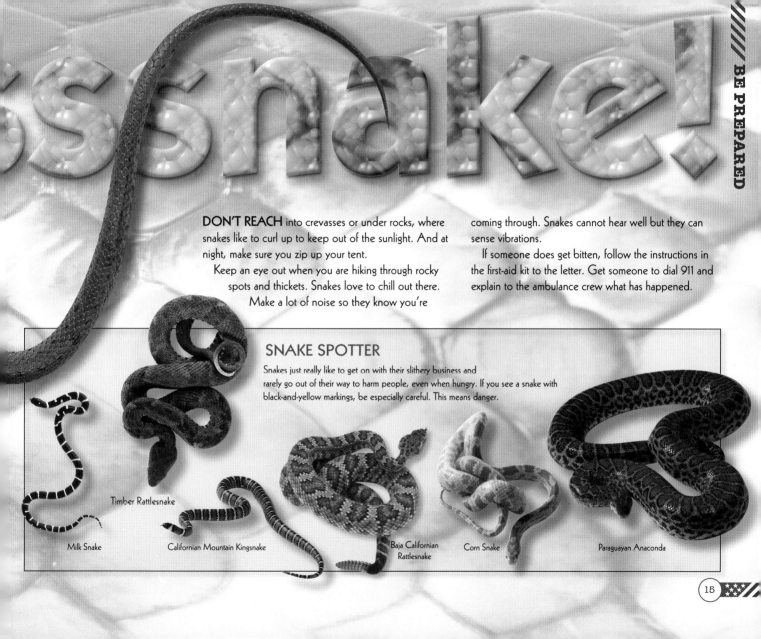

...s snake!

DON'T REACH into crevasses or under rocks, where snakes like to curl up to keep out of the sunlight. And at night, make sure you zip up your tent.

Keep an eye out when you are hiking through rocky spots and thickets. Snakes love to chill out there. Make a lot of noise so they know you're coming through. Snakes cannot hear well but they can sense vibrations.

If someone does get bitten, follow the instructions in the first-aid kit to the letter. Get someone to dial 911 and explain to the ambulance crew what has happened.

SNAKE SPOTTER

Snakes just really like to get on with their slithery business and rarely go out of their way to harm people, even when hungry. If you see a snake with black-and-yellow markings, be especially careful. This means danger.

Milk Snake

Timber Rattlesnake

Californian Mountain Kingsnake

Baja Californian Rattlesnake

Corn Snake

Paraguayan Anaconda

play a game of marbles

Marrididdles, **cat's eyes**, **alleys**, and **taws**...say what? Those are all names for different types and sizes of marbles. Kids have played marbles for thousands of years. Marble games were popular in ancient Rome and Egypt, and even Shakespeare wrote about a marble game. Why not grab a handful of these glassy goodies, gather up your friends, and put a new spin on this old game? Just make sure you don't lose your marbles while you're at it...

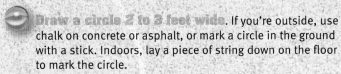

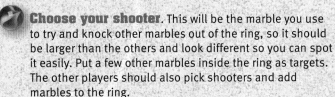

MARBLE WORDS

Alley Nickname for your best or most prized marble

Cat's eyes Beautiful marbles made of clear glass with colored glass injected inside them

Keepsies Game in which players keep all the marbles they win (make sure everyone agrees before you play keepsies!)

Marrididdles Homemade marbles, usually made by rolling clay into balls and letting them dry

Taw Name for your favorite shooter

Draw a circle 2 to 3 feet wide. If you're outside, use chalk on concrete or asphalt, or mark a circle in the ground with a stick. Indoors, lay a piece of string down on the floor to mark the circle.

Choose your shooter. This will be the marble you use to try and knock other marbles out of the ring, so it should be larger than the others and look different so you can spot it easily. Put a few other marbles inside the ring as targets. The other players should also pick shooters and add marbles to the ring.

Take turns shooting your marbles from outside the ring at any of the marbles inside the ring. To do this, kneel down with your shooter held in your fist, resting on the crook of your index finger. Put your index-finger knuckle on the ground, and flick your shooter out with your thumb. If you knock a marble out of the ring, it's your prize. Take it, and take another turn. (If you don't, it's time for the next player to try his luck.)

Keep playing until the ring is empty. Count your marbles. The player with the most wins the game. These are the basic rules, but there are countless variations. Why not think up a few variations with your friends, to customize your marbles game?

- Write down your assignments in a homework journal so they are easy to keep track of. Make sure to include the due date. (If your assignment isn't due for a few days, you may be tempted to leave it until the last minute. Try to avoid this...the homework might take you much longer than you think it will.)

- Find a quiet place to do your homework, where you won't be distracted. When you finish, you can be as distracted as you like! It's also a good idea to get in the habit of setting aside a specific time (like the hour before dinner) to do your assignments, every school day.

- Don't put off a difficult assignment so you can do the easy ones first. Dive right in and get started, then you can finish the easy stuff quickly at the end.

- Take breaks so your brain gets a rest.

- Reward yourself! If you're finding it hard to get motivated, promise yourself 15 minutes of free time after you finally manage to get to the bottom of the worksheet.

To Do List

22 Feb: start math homework.

23 Feb: finish math homework.

24 Feb: MATH HOMEWORK DUE

27 Feb: guitar practice.

28 Feb: wash football kit.

1 MAR: GUITAR CONCERT.

4 MAR: start Spanish homework.

8 Mar: finish spanish homework.

10 Mar: Spanish HOMEWORK DUE.

HOW TO HANDLE YOUR HOMEWORK

BE A LOYAL FRIEND

HOW WOULD YOU DESCRIBE YOUR BEST FRIEND? ALWAYS THERE FOR YOU.... SOMEONE YOU CAN DEPEND ON...FUN TO BE AROUND...REALLY UNDERSTANDS YOU...OWES YOU TEN BUCKS FOR THAT MOVIE TICKET? A GOOD FRIEND IS A GOOD THING TO HAVE. HERE'S HOW TO BE ONE—AND HOW TO KEEP ONE.

BE YOURSELF

SPEND TIME WITH EACH OTHER

BE RESPECTFUL

DON'T MAKE PROMISES YOU CAN'T KEEP

KEEP EACH OTHER'S SECRETS

SHARE YOUR LAST STICK OF GUM

HAVE FUN! BE REAL

LISTEN TO EACH OTHER

PITCH IN WHEN THERE'S A CRISIS

WATCH OUT FOR EACH OTHER

LAUGH AS MUCH AS YOU CAN

GIVE EACH OTHER SPACE

LET EACH OTHER HAVE OTHER FRIENDS

BE HAPPY FOR EACH OTHER

DON'T STAY MAD AT EACH OTHER

MAKE A SUPER-COOL SCARECROW

IF YOU GROW YOUR OWN FRUITS AND VEGGIES, and don't exactly want to share them with the birds, you might want to build one of these fake farmhands for your garden. They might just keep hungry birds at bay. You can make them as scary or as friendly as you like.

STUFF YOU NEED:

For a human-sized scarecrow, two lengths of bamboo pole or thick wooden dowel, one about 6 feet long and the other about 4 feet long

Garden twine, strong household string, or florist's wire—whatever's handy

Old clothes: shirt, gloves, trousers or skirt, hat, belt, pantyhose or a pillowcase to make the head

Straw, dry leaves, or even more old clothes for stuffing

Rubber bands

Felt tip pens or paint, to make a face

Active imagination!

If you're putting your scarecrow in your garden, ask an adult to help you push the pole firmly into the ground. You could dangle a couple of foil pie-plates, washed cans, or old CDs from the scarecrow's arms. The noise they make clanging together in the wind, and the light they reflect, can scare birds away.

WHAT TO DO

Lay down the longer pole and place the shorter one across it about a foot from the top. Tie or wire them together. This will be the body and arms of your scarecrow.

TO DRESS YOUR SCARECROW: Put an old shirt on the frame and button it up, then stuff it with your chosen stuffing. Stick the pole through one leg of an old pair of trousers (the other will hang free.) Tie off the trousers at the ankles with rubber bands or string, and stuff the legs lightly. Tuck the shirt in...you don't want a sloppy scarecrow, do you? Hold the trousers to the pole with an old belt or more string. Make a head for your creation by stuffing a pillowcase or an old pair of pantyhose, and draw on a face. Place it on top of the pole and secure at the "neck" with string. Top it all off with an old hat.

Do rats get sweaty?

GO TO PAGE 72

HAVE A BRUTALLY CLEAN ROOM

GO FOR IT: pick up all the trash and put it in a bag. You are setting aside any recyclable stuff, right? Good. Now, get everything out in the open. Look behind desks, under the bed, on top of the bookshelves… everywhere, really. Put it in a big pile in the middle of the room. You're probably thinking: "hang on a second—I'm supposed to be cleaning, not making a bigger mess." But watching the size of the pile go down as you put things away is a real motivator. There should be nowhere left for clutter to hide.

The first thing to tackle is the dirty clothes. Pick them up and put them in the laundry basket (or wherever dirty clothes live in your place). If you find clean stuff, hang it up or fold it and put it away. Your closet and drawers will look tidier if the doors are shut and things aren't sticking out.

What you need: a seriously messy room. Got that? Thought so. A trash bag is a good call, too.

Before you begin: **Step away from your computer. You might even consider turning it off. You don't want any pings distracting you from the task at hand, do you? (It's probably a good idea, though, to put on some music. Anything that fires you up will work.)**

Stack stuff **up neatly. This might be an amazing surprise to you, but everything has a place. (By the way, that place isn't back under the bed.)**

Change your **sheets and (gasp!) make the bed.**

Tidy up **your desk or computer area—computers really do attract dust—and dust everything with a duster or cloth. Bookshelves are another dust magnet, so give those a little attention, too.**

Now run **the vacuum cleaner to pick up all the dust you've shifted. Make sure you get the spot between the bed and the wall. Please don't vacuum up any socks that might be lingering there.**

Next wipe **down surfaces with a wet cloth. Almost there!**

Open up **the curtains or blinds and let the sun shine in to your amazingly clean room.**

HOW TO CLIMB A TREE

THERE ARE SOME TREES THAT ARE JUST MADE FOR CLIMBING. CLAMBERING UP THE BRANCHES OF A PERFECT CLIMBING TREE IS AMAZINGLY GOOD FUN (EVEN IF COMING BACK DOWN CAN BE A LITTLE SCARY.) TO BE ON THE SAFE SIDE, YOU SHOULD CLIMB WITH AN ADULT WHO STAYS ON THE GROUND.

1. PICK A WINNER

Scout out a tree with branches thick and sturdy enough to take your weight. Watch out for saggy branches or lots of broken ones on the ground—the tree might not be healthy and strong enough to climb safely. Look for a tree with lots of branches together—not so far apart that you get stuck.

2. GOING UP!

Look for a good, solid place to put your foot or hand, and step or lift yourself up. You can use gnarly knots, holes, and smaller branches as footholds. Watch out for any crumbly or rotten branches. You can test them first by pressing down with your foot to see if they give. Keep your movements steady and strong as you climb. When you run out of branches—or when you get as far up as you feel comfortable go-ing—stop and enjoy the view!

3. DOWN TIME

Be really careful coming down the tree. Take your time and resist the urge to jump. If your foot slips a little, grab a branch so you don't end up sliding down the trunk. Most times it is easier to come down facing the tree than with your back to its trunk. When you're safely down, why not challenge your buddy to make the climb, while you spot for him? Or, you could branch out a little, and look for a taller tree to scamper up.

CAUTION!
DON'T ATTEMPT TO CLIMB A TREE WITHOUT ADULT SUPERVISION!

Who invented the tin can?

ABSOLUTELY

What could possibly be better than a good joke? That's easy: a really bad joke. A groaner, a moaner, total no-hoper. Like these.

PAINFUL ANIMAL JOKES

WHICH SIDE OF A CHICKEN HAS THE MOST FEATHERS?

The outside.

WHAT HAPPENS WHEN A FROG BREAKS DOWN?

It gets toad away.

WHAT'S ORANGE AND SOUNDS LIKE A PARROT?

A carrot.

HOW MANY SKUNKS DOES IT TAKE TO MAKE A BIG STINK?

A phew.

WHAT DO BEES CHEW?

Bumble gum.

WHAT DO YOU GET IF YOU SIT UNDER A COW?

A pat on the head.

AWFUL JOKES

USELESS SCHOOL JOKES

WHAT'S BLACK AND WHITE AND EXTREMELY DIFFICULT?
A test paper.

WHAT WAS THE BIRD DOING IN THE SCHOOL LIBRARY?
Looking for bookworms.

WHERE WAS THE DECLARATION OF INDEPENDENCE SIGNED?
At the bottom.

WHAT DID ONE MATH BOOK SAY TO THE OTHER?
Boy, have I got problems.

WHY WERE THE TEACHER'S EYES CROSSED?
He couldn't control his pupils.

UNFUNNY KNOCK-KNOCK JOKES

KNOCK, KNOCK.
Who's there?
ROMEO
Romeo who?
ROMEOVER THE RIVER.

KNOCK, KNOCK.
Who's there?
COWS GO.
Cows go who?
NO, COWS GO MOO.

KNOCK, KNOCK.
Who's there?
HEYWOOD.
Heywood who?
HEYWOOD YOU OPEN THE DOOR?

KNOCK, KNOCK.
Who's there?
REPEAT.
Repeat who?
WHO, WHO, WHO.

KNOCK, KNOCK.
Who's there?
YULE.
Yule who?
YULE NEVER KNOW.

KNOCK, KNOCK.
Who's there?
JUAN.
Juan who?
JUAN TO HEAR MORE JOKES?

MONUMENTALLY DUMB JOKES

What are microwaves? Tiny greetings.

WHAT'S ROUND, SAD, AND LIVES IN THE TRUNK OF YOUR CAR?
DE-SPAIR TIRE.

WHAT'S BROWN AND STICKY? A STICK.

What do you call a boomerang that doesn't come back? Also a stick.

What's round and bad-tempered? A vicious circle.

WHAT'S PINK AND DANGEROUS?

What's a twack? Something a twain runs on.

WHAT TWO **WORDS** HAVE THE MOST LETTERS? POST OFFICE.

WHAT INVENTION ALLOWS PEOPLE TO SEE THROUGH WALLS? WINDOWS.

WHAT DO YOU CALL A MAN WITH A SEAGULL ON HIS HEAD? CLIFF.

WHAT'S YELLOW ON THE OUTSIDE AND GREEN ON THE INSIDE? A CUCUMBER DRESSED AS A BANANA.

WHY DID THE BEE GO TO THE DOCTOR? BECAUSE IT HAD HIVES.

SHARK-INFESTED STRAWBERRY ICE CREAM.

BEAR HUG

While it's true that not every hike in bear country leads to a terrifying bear hug, it's good to know what to do in case of a close encounter. Bears are generally timid and will keep away from humans if they can. But how you handle the meeting could stop the bear from handling you!

Don't surprise a bear—let it know you are there. Hike in a group and stay out in the open where possible. Stay away from dead animals and other things that might attract a bear. Don't keep food in your tent if you're camping in bear country (hang it high in a tree or keep it in a really secure container instead), and dispose of your trash carefully. (And while we're at it, never feed wild bears. Not only is it illegal in lots of places, it helps bears lose their fear of human beings...something that doesn't bear thinking about!)

In the extremely unlikely event that the bear should suddenly charge, you could try to play dead. As a last resort, try to intimidate the bear in whatever way you can.

SURVIVAL ESSENTIALS?

If you do see a bear, keep well away.
1. Don't look the bear in the eyes, or do anything that shows aggression.
2. Keep your voice quiet and calm and your movements slow and steady as you move away.
3. Do not scream and run away, as much as you may want to do exactly that. Bears can run at least twice as fast as you can.

TUG OF WAR

What you need: a length of rope (a rope about 30 feet long, made of natural fibers is best), duct tape, measuring tape, a bandanna and plenty of people. Choose a large, flat, grassy area to play on. Mark a spot on the ground with duct tape. This will be the center line.

Find the center of the rope and tie a bandanna (or tape) around it. Use tape to make two marks, 10 feet either side of the bandanna.

Divide into teams of an equal number, and face each other, with the center of the rope over the center line. Pick up the rope and pull like you've never pulled before, to try and get the mark on your opponent's side of the rope to cross the center line.

HAND SHADOW PUPPETS

Create these cool illusions against a white or light-colored wall in a darkened room. Put a lantern behind you so that you can throw spooky shadows, or ask a friend to aim his flashlight your way. (Nice of him to give you a hand, isn't it?) With a little practice you can make some truly amazing shadow puppets—a handy little way to have fun!

Bird in flight

Dog

Dinosaur

Bat

How many meteoroids rain down on Earth each day?

GO TO PAGE 55

SEVEN SUPER-COOL THINGS TO DO IN THE SNOW

BUILD AN IGLOO

Mold snow "bricks" by packing snow tightly into a large container (a baking pan will work) and then set them in a circle, leaving space for a door. Add another ring just behind the first. Next, add another row of bricks along the inside rim of the bottom row, so the walls look as if they slope. Keep going until the tops of the walls touch together. Your igloo is a great place to chill.

SNOW? WHAT SNOW?

Go outside and do something you'd usually do in the summer. Try riding your bike (it's super tricky), playing a game of football (one fumble and you tumble), shooting some hoops, or even blowing soap bubbles in the frosty air. Don't wear your flip-flops, though!

SNOWFLAKE STUDY

Put some black construction paper in the freezer for a couple of hours (yes, that is a little weird but trust us) and when it's really cold, take it outside and catch a few snowflakes. Look at their amazing patterns with a magnifying glass.

SNOWBALL TARGET PRACTICE

Roll up a big pile of snowballs, pick a tough target to hit, like a skinny tree or a distant fence post, take ten steps back, and let fly. How many times can you hit the tree in ten tries? Step back ten more steps. How's your aim now?

FROZEN TAG

Playing a game of tag in the snow provides plenty of chances for thrills, chills, and spills. Want to make it even harder? Play footsteps tag. No one can take a step into fresh snow—they can only walk in someone else's footprints.

SNOWY SCAVENGER HUNT

Hide five waterproof items in the snow, and create a treasure map for your friends to follow. First one to find everything gets a mug of hot chocolate.

SNOW SCULPTURE

Raid the kitchen for an assortment of plastic bowls and molds, ice-cream scoops, and baking pans. Use them to mold the snow into different shapes and create a sensational snow sculpture.

P.S.

S'no day like a snow day to do a good deed. Pull a little kid around on a sled, or show him or her how to make the perfect snow angel or a top-notch snowball. If there's someone in your neighborhood who can't get around easily, offer to shovel the front steps or sidewalk. Offer to do a grocery-store run for someone who's shut inside.

OPEN A BANK ACCOUNT

YOU'RE A BIG KID NOW, AND THE PIGGY BANK JUST WON'T DO THE JOB ANY MORE. SAVING MONEY IS AN IMPORTANT SKILL TO LEARN AND THE RIGHT BANK ACCOUNT CAN HELP YOU GROW YOUR SAVINGS.

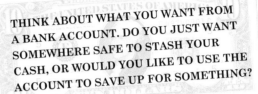

THINK ABOUT WHAT YOU WANT FROM A BANK ACCOUNT. DO YOU JUST WANT SOMEWHERE SAFE TO STASH YOUR CASH, OR WOULD YOU LIKE TO USE THE ACCOUNT TO SAVE UP FOR SOMETHING?

CHECK OUT THE BANKS IN YOUR TOWN AND FIND OUT WHAT SORTS OF DEALS OR OFFERS THEY HAVE FOR CHILDREN'S ACCOUNTS. (DON'T BE TOO TEMPTED WHEN BANKS OFFER STUFF FOR FREE WHEN YOU OPEN A NEW ACCOUNT. YOU MIGHT END UP PAYING FOR THAT GIFT THROUGH BANK FEES.) ASK FOR PAPERWORK.

YEP, NOW IT'S TIME TO READ THE FINE PRINT! FIND OUT WHAT INTEREST THE BANK OFFERS TO SAVERS (THAT'S MONEY THEY PAY TO YOU, WHEN YOU AGREE TO LET THE BANK KEEP YOUR CASH) AND WHAT CHARGES THEY MAKE (THAT'S MONEY YOU PAY TO THEM.)

WHEN YOU'VE FOUND A BANK THAT YOU FEEL OFFERS A GOOD DEAL, ASK YOUR PARENTS WHAT THEY THINK. IT'S A GOOD IDEA TO INVOLVE THEM, AND YOU'LL SHOW THEM YOU ARE SERIOUS ABOUT LEARNING HOW TO HANDLE MONEY. WHO KNOWS...THEY MIGHT EVEN OFFER YOU A LITTLE SOMETHING TO PUT IN YOUR NEW ACCOUNT.

The INTERNET is an incredibly cool tool. But as with any tool, you have to know what you're doing when you use it, and always put safety first. There are some pretty shady characters hanging out on the Information Highway . . . Here are some tips to help you zoom right by them, surfing safely into the sunset.

HOW TO BE SAFE

Don't open attachments from people you don't know. They might be sneaking a virus or spyware through. Talk to your parents before you download software, or do anything that might possibly put your computer at risk.

Everyone has an opinion, and it seems like almost everyone's put that opinion on line. But if someone is nasty or insulting, or throws out more flames than a bonfire, don't talk to them anymore.

If you come across material that makes you uncomfortable, please tell your parents.

If you subscribe to lots of websites, you might consider doing so through a freebie account, instead of your regular web address. That way, if a site sells your name on to another, your e-mail account won't be clogged up with junk mail.

ON THE INTERNET!

Safeguard your computer with a firewall, a good anti-virus program, and spyware remover.

If someone makes you feel uncomfortable or asks you to do something that you feel is wrong, tell your parents. Don't respond. Turn your computer off.

If you are hooked on instant messaging, make sure you go to the preferences menu and choose the settings that offer you the highest level of security. Keep your profile private on social networking sites.

Change your password from time to time and don't give it to anyone no matter what (except your parents.) Try a really weird password (mixing up letters and numbers and punctuation) to make it super tough to guess. Don't use the same password over and over to log onto sites—passwords are secrets, and when you tell more than one computer your secret, it isn't a secret anymore!

37

FLING A FLYING DISK FAR, FAR, AWAY

If you're right-handed, stand with your right shoulder facing your target. (If you're left-handed, do the reverse.) The way you hold the flying disk is key: put your index finger on the curvy part, your middle, ring, and little fingers on the inside rim, and rest your thumb on top.

Now off you go. Curl your arm in and then uncurl it, letting go of the disk right before your arm is fully extended. Try to keep the disk level, as if you are balancing a glass of water on it.

To catch a flying disk, clap your hands together as the disk flies in between them. Careful—a fast-moving disk can hurt your fingers.

Dot, dot, dash! Fun with a flash

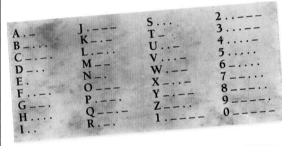

A .-	J .---	S ...	2 ..---
B -...	K -.-	T -	3 ...--
C -.-.	L .-..	U ..-	4 ....-
D -..	M --	V ...-	5 .....
E .	N -.	W .--	6 -....
F ..-.	O ---	X -..-	7 --...
G --.	P .--.	Y -.--	8 ---..
H	Q --.-	Z --..	9 ----.
I ..	R .-.	1 .----	0 -----

Morse Code was created as a way to send messages using short and long bursts of sound, marks on paper, or flashes of light. The short elements are known as dots and the long ones as dashes. The code was developed by American inventor Samuel F. B. Morse in the 1830s. He hit upon the idea of representing numbers and letters through a code based on short and long pulses of electricity. Study the alphabet in this chart, and try sending a message by flashing long and short bursts of light.

You wouldn't think of packing a camp kit without a flashlight. It's a handy and portable light source. It's also the source of some serious fun. You can send messages to each other in flashlight Morse Code. Make sure you've got a spare bulb and fresh batteries, and you're off...and on...and off...

More flashlight fun

Flashlight tag is an excellent game to play after the sun goes down. It's more challenging when you can play in a large area, like a park or playing field. Everyone needs a flashlight. To begin, pair off and decide a team signal (two short flashes of light, one long and three short, etc.) Players are given one minute to get as far away from their partners as they possibly can. When the minute is up, they can begin flashing signals while looking out for their signaling partners. The first team to reunite wins the game.

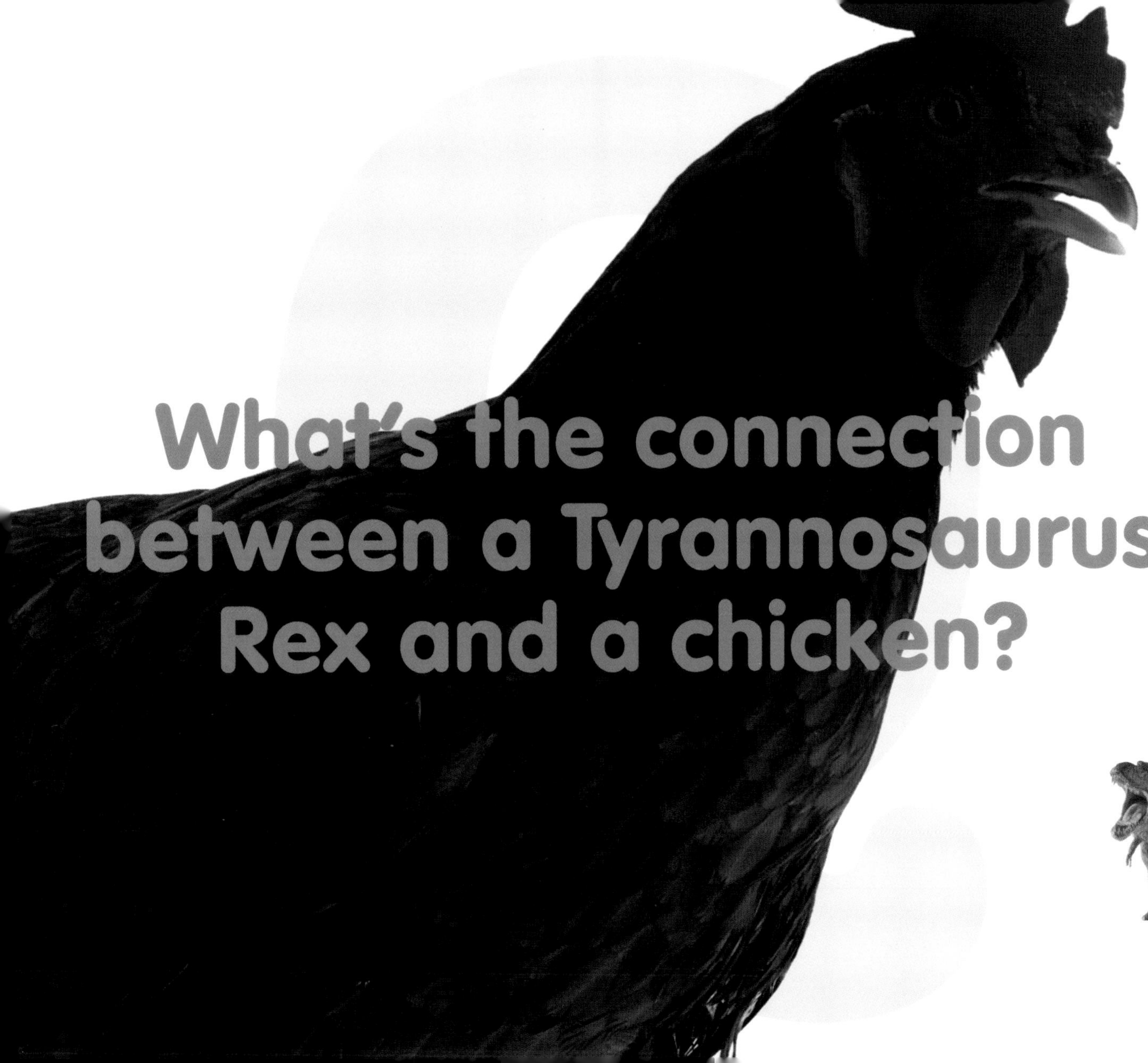

GO TO PAGE 57

What's the connection between a Tyrannosaurus Rex and a chicken?

39

Maybe it's not likely that you will cross paths with a mountain lion today. But then again, maybe today is not your lucky day...

BIG CAT

MOUNTAIN LIONS are America's largest wild cats. These powerful predators are on the prowl in increasing numbers, in the western part of the United States. When hiking or camping in the wilderness, it's always a good idea to know what to do in case you encounter a big cat. The most important advice is to keep your head and be aware of what's going on around you. Like any predators, mountain lions look for easy prey. Make

5'0"

4'6"

4'0"

3'6"

3'0"

Bobcat

Leopard cat

Lynx

sure that's not going to be you. If you do see a mountain lion, don't suddenly turn and run (mountain lions are excellent at running down their prey), play dead, or make sudden loud noises that might trigger an attack. Stay as calm as you possibly can. Maintain eye contact with the cat as you make yourself look as large as possible. Lift your arms up and open your jacket. If you can, climb onto something, but don't turn your back on the cat. Bare your teeth and growl. If the cat attacks, fight with all you've got. Throw rocks, use a stick, and be resourceful. The rules are, there are no rules! Plenty of people (even kids) have fought off big cat attacks.

SURVIVAL ESSENTIALS?

To avoid meeting a mountain lion in the first place, follow basic safety rules:

1. Keep a clean camp.
2. Don't hike alone.
3. Try to stay in open areas.
4. Always use a flashlight at night (so the mountain lion can see you and move away.)

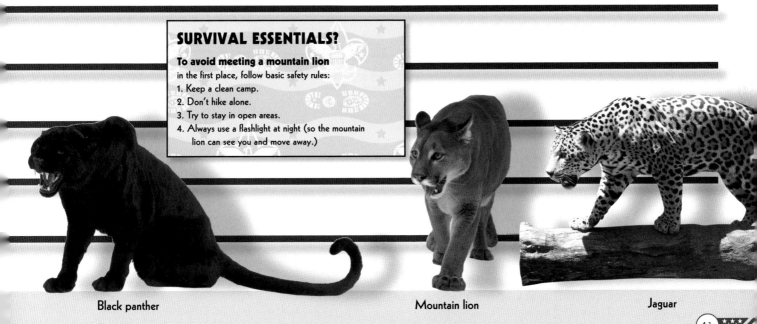

Black panther

Mountain lion

Jaguar

GO TO PAGE 121

How many dreams will I dream?

Hostage!
Hostage!
Hostage!
Hostage!

You will need: Kids, kids, and more kids.

This game is a lot like Capture the Flag, with a cool twist. Split into two teams and decide where each team's territory begins and ends. You'll also need to mark a "jail" for each team. Then, each team will select a hostage from the other side, and exchange them. The teams will hide the hostage somewhere in their territory. At the start signal, each team will try to rescue their hostage. Some people will stay in their area to guard their captive, while others will try to invade enemy territory to release the hostage. But beware! If you are tagged in enemy territory, you must go to jail. The only way out of jail is if a teammate rescues you. The team that rescues the hostage wins.

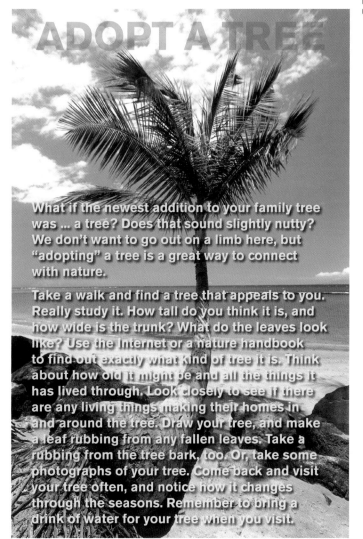

ADOPT A TREE

What if the newest addition to your family tree was ... a tree? Does that sound slightly nutty? We don't want to go out on a limb here, but "adopting" a tree is a great way to connect with nature.

Take a walk and find a tree that appeals to you. Really study it. How tall do you think it is, and how wide is the trunk? What do the leaves look like? Use the Internet or a nature handbook to find out exactly what kind of tree it is. Think about how old it might be and all the things it has lived through. Look closely to see if there are any living things making their homes in and around the tree. Draw your tree, and make a leaf rubbing from any fallen leaves. Take a rubbing from the tree bark, too. Or, take some photographs of your tree. Come back and visit your tree often, and notice how it changes through the seasons. Remember to bring a drink of water for your tree when you visit.

My Notes

about absolutely anything

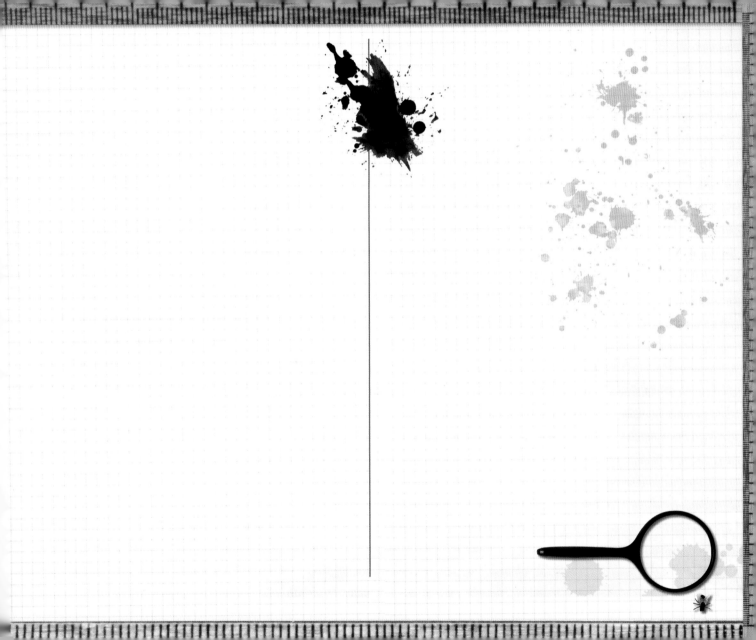

Ornithology

Bird	Study
1 Passenger jet. *Go to pages 12-13*	13 Northern goshawk
2 Frigatebird	14 Black-headed gull
3 Eastern rosella	15 Blackbird
4 Robin	16 Chaffinch
5 Red-tailed minla	17 Common kestrel
6 Eurasian jay	18 Pigeon
7 Blue budgerigar	19 Seagull
8 Sparkling violet-ear	20 Jackdaw
9 Red-winged starling	21 Saddle-billed stork
10 Canary-winged parakeet	22 Green woodpecker
11 Snowy owl	23 Pigeon
12 Barn owl	24 Tawny eagle

Notes

Keeping track of everything.

BE SAFE, WHEREVER YOU ARE

SMASHES AND CRASHES. BOO-BOOS, AND BLUNDERS. MISHAPS AND MESS-UPS. ACCIDENTS HAPPEN–THAT'S A GIVEN. (WHY ELSE WOULD THEY HAVE INVENTED BANDAGES?) BUT IF YOU FOLLOW A FEW SAFETY GUIDELINES, YOU MAY BE ABLE TO PREVENT THE WORST. THERE'S USUALLY A SAFER WAY TO DO MOST THINGS. (AND IF YOU DO COMPLETELY FLUB A SKATEBOARD TRICK OR TRIP OVER AN "INVISIBLE" CRACK IN THE SIDEWALK, TRY TO LAUGH. LIKE SOMEONE ALWAYS SEEMS TO SAY WHEN YOU STUMBLE: "HAVE A NICE TRIP! SEE YOU NEXT FALL!"

SCHOOL SAFETY

Know the rules of your school and follow them.

School bus riders should learn the rules for safe boarding and exiting the bus. If you have to cross the road in front of the bus, please use caution, and make sure the driver is aware of you at all times.

Don't goof around on the bus–the driver needs to concentrate.

If you walk to school, follow the traffic laws and cross at crossings.

When you arrive at school, use the designated loading zones.

TRAVEL SAFETY

If you ride a bicycle, keep your bike in good working order, always wear a bicycle helmet, and follow all the safety rules and traffic signals.

Avoid cycling or walking at night. Even if you are using a bike light or are wearing reflective clothing, it's harder for drivers to see you in the dark.

When walking, always cross at crossings and pay attention to signs and signals. Stay alert, use your eyes and ears, and you'll stay safe.

Help your parents install smoke and carbon monoxide detectors in your home and make sure to test the batteries regularly.

Look after your brothers and sisters, and help keep them out of danger.

Know a neighbor who will lend you a hand if need be.

Be careful where you play. Stairs and landings can be dangerous. (Make sure you de-clutter stairs and other areas where people could trip and fall.)

Keep a list of emergency numbers by the phone: police, fire, ambulance, and poison control center.

Please be really careful with boiling water and hot drinks; they are a common cause of household burns and scalds.

If you live in an area where there are other risks—for example, earthquakes, tornadoes, and hurricanes—study the safety rules and make sure your whole family knows what to do in an emergency.

Work with your family to create an escape plan in case of fire. Everyone should know what to do. You probably have lots of fire drills at school—why not suggest one at home?

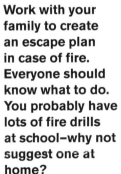

SAFETY AT HOME

Put together a first-aid kit and make sure everyone knows where it is. Contents of a typical kit include: adhesive and roller bandages, antiseptic wipes (cream or spray), alcohol swabs, a gel pad for burns, a large triangular bandage, plastic tape, latex gloves, soap or hand sanitizer, and a flashlight. If someone in your family is allergic to insect bites or stings, ask your doctor for an emergency kit.

MY NOTES

SAFETY RULES AT HOME AND AT SCHOOL

SCHOOL BUS STOP AHEAD

35 M.P.H.

BE SAFE,
WHEREVER
YOU ARE

ONE
WAY
→

Make the most super soak-tastic water balloons ever

You can use other kinds of balloon, but ones sold as water balloons are the best to buy as they are made to reach the perfect size for lobbing when filled.

Use only clean tap water to fill your balloons. Stretch the open end of the balloon to fit over the tap and turn on the water. Use one hand to hold the balloon onto the tap and the other to support the balloon as it stretches out and fills.

Don't overfill your balloon bombs (or else, splat! Soaked shoes.) A grapefruit size is about right. Leave enough room at the top so you can tie the balloon shut and still squeeze it a little.

A plastic bag is the best way to transport filled balloons. If any do pop, the mess will be contained.

Take aim and let the soaking begin! When the water fight is over, clean up the mess. Little kids and animals might ingest the balloon fragments, so leave the battlezone tidy.

PLAYING A GAME OF CATCH WITH WATER BALLOONS IS A COOL WAY TO GET DRENCHED ON A HOT SUMMER DAY.

let me twist your arm

Maybe you've been told to keep your elbows off the table, but it's the only way to win an arm-wrestling match. Sit on either side of a table or other surface facing your opponent.

Each person puts one arm on the surface, elbows bent and touching the table. Grip each other's hand. Now try to pin the other person's arm down on the table, keeping your elbows on its surface. **May the best arm-twister win!**

How about a thumb-wrestle? Face each other, and hook the four fingers of your left (or right) hand together with the four fingers of your opponent's opposite hand. At the starting signal, try to pin down your opponent's thumb with yours for three seconds, while wriggling your own thumb to evade being squashed by his! Who will get the thumbs-up...and who gets the thumbs down?

Each and every day, even Tuesdays, up to 4 billion meteoroids enter Earth's atmosphere. But you can leave your umbrella at home—most of them are teeny, tiny specks of space dust.

MAKE YOUR OWN SIDEWALK CHALK

Could you be the Da Vinci of your driveway? Do you want to turn your same-old sidewalk into an art gallery? Why not make your own sidewalk chalk, and let your inner artist go outside?

STUFF YOU NEED:
- Plaster of Paris • Powdered tempera paint in assorted colors • Water • An old mixing bowl • An old wooden spoon • Molds for your chalk—such as small paper cups, yogurt cups, toilet paper rolls, an old plastic popsicle mold set, or an ice-cube tray.

WHAT TO DO:
Set up your molds in an out-of-the-way place. A corner of the garage or a patio will do. It may take a few days for your chalk to dry out, so don't put them slap-bang in the middle of somewhere.

Mix one cup plaster of Paris with one cup of water. Shake in tempera paint to color the mixture. Let it stand for a few minutes.

Now pour the mixture into the molds. Let it dry completely.

Unmold the chalk and let it dry for another day to harden. Now make your masterpiece. Use your chalk to draw a dazzling display of sidewalk art for the whole neighborhood to see —until the next time it rains.

It's hard to believe, but they are related. Birds (and that includes chickens) evolved from dinosaurs. Scientists studied a 68-million-year-old T-rex bone and found it was almost an exact match to that of a modern chicken.

Will you crack the clues and find the treasure? Setting up a treasure hunt is almost as much fun as playing one. The basics of the game involve getting a clue that leads you to a certain place, then finding another clue there that leads you to another place, and finally finding the last clue that leads to a treasure. There are all kinds of ways to set up a cool treasure hunt. Here is a treasure trove of hints and ideas to get you started. Happy hunting…

Make sure the clues are not too hard or too easy, and that there aren't too many of them. As a guideline, if ten-year-olds are hunting, write ten clues to get to the treasure.

You might want to write down a copy of the clues, and list where you've hidden them, in case you forget (or your clues are so fiendishly clever no one can figure them out.)

If the weather is awful, set up an indoor treasure hunt. For an extra challenge, write the clues in code. Players will have to crack the code to find the treasure.

Set up a Tantalizing Treasure Hunt

book kerlies jewels

00.00 o.a.s.i.s

3

*I*f you don't mind a bit of a mess, try a disgusting and gross treasure hunt. Put the clues in sealed sandwich bags, then hide them in yucky places: under a pile of cold spaghetti, in an unwashed sock, somewhere really dusty, and so on.

*I*f your parents are OK with it (and please check with them first), there is nothing quite so exciting as finding buried treasure. Put the final clue in a matchbox or small plastic tub before you bury it. You could also hide treasure in the sand at a local park.

*H*old a flashlight treasure hunt on a summer night. It's a good idea to pair up and use the buddy system if you are doing anything at night, and stay well away from roads and cars.

*S*et up a compass treasure hunt for your troop. Give clues as compass bearings, with the distance in steps to the next clue. You can brush up on your orienteering skills and have fun at the same time.

*H*ow about a bicycle treasure hunt? Your friends will pedal to a certain location, solve a riddle, then zoom off to the next spot. Map out a route, write clues based on local landmarks. On your bikes, you're off!

AMAZING

Arthropods are amazing animals. They are everywhere. Over 80 percent of the animals on Earth are arthropods. Here are just a few that you might see.

Arachnids

COMMON TICK

RED DEER TICK

HOUSE SPIDER

BANANA SPIDER

MEXICAN RED-KNEED SPIDER

DESERT SCORPION

IMPERIAL SCORPION

Millipedes and centipedes

PILL MILLIPEDE

MILLIPEDE ROLLED UP

ARMORED MILLIPEDE

CENTIPEDE

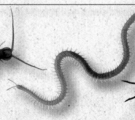

MILLIPEDE

GIANT TIGER CENTIPEDE

Insects

PIERROT BUTTERFLY

PERICOPINE MOTH

BROWNTAIL MOTH

ILIA UNDERWING MOTH

ARTHROPODS

jointed

feet

Crustaceans

FRESHWATER
CRAYFISH

SPIDER CRAB

CRAB

PRAWNS

GOOSE BARNACLES

BLACK LOBSTER

QUEEN ALEXANDRA'S BIRD-
WING BUTTERFLY

WATER BEETLE

SILVER BEETLE

DUNG BEETLE

HOVER FLY

PRAYING MANTIS

STAG BEETLE

HORSEFLY

COLLECT FIREFLIES

They slip silently through the skies on a summer night, their yellow glow blinking on and off. Have you ever wondered why fireflies flash their lights? Lightning bugs, also called fireflies, are not insects nor flies, but a type of beetle. They glow because they are trying to attract mates.

In most species, the males fly around flashing their abdominal lights while females perch nearby, in or near the ground. Each species of firefly (there are around 136 different ones) has its own flash pattern, from continuous glowing to a series of on-off flashes. It's a little like Morse code (see page 38) for beetles! If a female recognizes a male of her species, and she's ready to mate, she flashes her light to attract the male's attention. When he notices her, he flashes back and moves closer. Through a series of flashes they eventually find each other and mate.

The female's eggs are laid a few days after mating, in or under the soil or tree bark. In about a month, they hatch into larvae, and begin to feed (they are carnivores) until fall. They burrow underground for the winter and emerge in the spring of the next year. They spend the spring gobbling up other insects, snails, or small animals living in the soil. When summer arrives, they are adults, ready to twinkle through the evening skies looking for a mate.

How many species of firefly do you have in your backyard? By noting the number of flashes and how long they last, you can work out how many there are.

2 Make a collection jar. Ask an adult to help you punch holes in the lid of a large Mason jar with a hammer and nails. These are air holes for the fireflies.

1

STUFF YOU NEED

A MASON JAR with lid

HAMMER and nails

STOPWATCH for timing

PENCIL AND PAPER to observe your findings

3 Gently catch a few fireflies and observe them. for about five minutes, recording the frequency and length of their flashes. Then return to the place you collected the fireflies and let them go free.

4 After an hour or so, go back to where you found the fireflies, and carefully capture some more. Observe them. Have you found a different species?

A male won't answer back if a female sends the wrong species signal. But some females have learned to mimic the flashes of a species other than their own. When the male flies down to her, he is eaten!

SNOWBALL FIGHT!

CHECK THE CHILL

Read your thermometer or check out the local weather forecast. The best temperature for snowball fights is right around freezing (32 degrees). If it's any warmer, the snow might be too moist to stick well.

KNOW YOUR SNOW

Just as no two snowflakes are alike, so no two snowballs are alike. The ideal snow is moist enough to make snowballs that hold together until they reach their target. If there's loads of snow on the ground, dig underneath the surface a little to get to the snow beneath. It's already been slightly packed already, so it will be easier to make into snowballs. When the temperature plunges below the freezing mark, the snow tends to be powdery and dry because of its low moisture content. If you're brave enough to venture out, look for a warmer spot (near a house, for example) to find snow that will pack well.

MITTENS VS. GLOVES

Gloves win hands-down when it comes to snowball fighting. You'll need all five fingers to shape super snowballs and sling them with accuracy. So, hands off the mittens for today.

THE PERFECT PACKAGE

Once you've found the right white stuff, it's time to get packing. Fill your cupped hands with snow, then gently close your hands together. Turn the snowball around in your hands as you squeeze them together to pack down the snow. When you cannot squeeze any more use your palms to gently shape the snow into a round ball. If you work too slowly, the heat of your hands might melt the snowball. With practice, you'll learn how to shape the most amazing snowballs ever.

LET 'EM FLY!

You can build up an arsenal of snowballs, or let them loose one at a time, as you make them. Keep your eyes on the prize, aim well, and throw that perfect snowball into the sky. Now that's what winter was made for.

Peter Durand, a British inventor, patented the tin can in 1810. The first can opener, however, wasn't patented until 1858. Go figure!

Write your town's biography

History isn't something that only happens in your school textbooks. Your own town, whether it is hundreds of years old or much younger, has its own unique story. There are lots of ways to find out about the people that built your community and hear their stories. With a little investigating, you can gather the facts and create the life story of your town. (Who knows? They might even put up a statue of you, if your story is really good....)

GO FOR A WALK: so you've probably walked, biked or skateboarded up and down the streets of your town thousands of times. But this time, you are a history detective. Look for clues from the past. Can you find any evidence of older buildings that came before existing ones? Who do you think named the city streets? Why was your town built where it is? Is it on a river, near a busy rail or road junction? What is the oldest part of town? Explore with fresh eyes, and you'll get inspired.

TRY THE LIBRARY: your local library will no doubt have a collection of books about local history in your area. The library might also hold photographs, maps, and original documents. Ask a librarian to point you in the right direction.

VISIT YOUR LOCAL ARCHIVES: almost every town, city, or county has a records or archives office containing a wealth of original documents and materials. Check the Internet to find yours, speak with someone about your project, and start digging for facts.

HISTORICAL SOCIETIES: *your town or county might already have a local history society. Its members are interested enough in local history to meet and do their own research, and no doubt you will find someone who will be happy to share information with you.*

VISIT THE LOCAL MUSEUM: *even if you've been there before visit again with fresh eyes. Ask the curator if you can have access to collections that may not be on display. You may find some exclusive stuff that makes your town biography one-of-a-kind.*

NOW YOU'VE GATHERED *all the facts, write down the true-life story of your town. You might want to start with a timeline or do it scrapbook-style. Add some extra stuff like copies of photos or important documents.*

HERPETOLOGY

STUDY OF

SNAKES

Some kids find snakes scary, but other kids love them. People who have a strong interest in herpetology (the study of reptiles and amphibians) and keep them as pets, call themselves "herpers."

Paraguayan Anaconda

Burmese Python

Timber Rattlesnake

Amphisbaena fuliginosa

Coiled Corn Snake

Calabar Ground Boa

Californian Mountain King snake

Burmese Python

Banded Milk Snake

Grass Snake

Thai Monocled Cobra

Green snake

Monocled Cobra

Royal Python

Common Adder

Common Milk Snake

Sonoran Mountain King Snake

Baird's Ratsnake

Diamondback Rattlesnake

Green Anaconda

fix a yummy
after-school snack

NUKED QUESADILLAS
(SERVES ONE)

2 6-inch flour or corn tortillas
¼ cup grated cheddar or Mexican-
  blend cheese mix
2 slices smoked turkey or ham
  (optional)
1 tbsp salsa

Veggies: sliced tomatoes, green or red peppers, drained canned corn niblets, chopped onion, or sliced black olives

1. Put one tortilla on a sheet of waxed paper and sprinkle on half the cheese. Top with turkey or ham and veggies of your choice, then sprinkle over the remaining cheese.
2. Slide the whole shebang onto a microwave-safe plate and cover with another sheet of waxed paper. Nuke on high for 1½–2 minutes or until the cheese melts. Keep an eye on things…stuff in the microwave can go from tasty to burned in a pretty short time. Let it cool for a couple of minutes, slice and enjoy.

ANTS ON A LOG
(SERVES TWO)

2 celery sticks, washed and trimmed
Jar of your favorite kind of peanut
  butter, chunky or smooth
Handful of raisins

1. Cut the celery sticks into finger-sized pieces on a cutting board. Watch your fingers…you don't want to end up with finger-sized pieces of fingers now, do you?
2. Use a table knife to fill the middle of the celery with peanut butter.
3. Add raisin "ants" and enjoy. If you aren't a peanut butter nut, you could also make these with cream cheese and celery. If celery bugs you, make ants on an apple with sliced apples, peanut butter, and raisins.

FREEZER FRUIT
(SERVES ONE)

A handful of green or red grapes
Sliced bananas
Melon balls

1. Wash and prepare the fruit and put it on a freezer-safe plate or in an ice-cube tray. Freeze overnight.
2. The next day, eat and enjoy. You won't believe how yummy frozen fruit can be.

DELUXE POPCORN TOPPERS

Season a piping-hot bag of microwave popcorn with one of the following:
¼ cup grated Parmesan cheese
½ tsp garlic powder and a sprinkle of paprika
1 to 2 tsp ranch salad dressing mix
½ tsp cinnamon mixed with 1 tsp sugar

VERY BERRY SMOOTHIE
(SERVES TWO)

1 cup orange juice
2 cups plain, low-fat yoghurt
¾ cup each washed and stemmed raspberries, blackberries, and blueberries
Honey to sweeten (you only need a little)

1. Put everything in a blender jar. Whatever you do, don't leave the lid off or you and everything around you will be covered in pulverized smoothie.
2. Blend at high speed until smooth. Pour into glasses and enjoy.

Ask an adult to help you use the blender.

EASY CHEESY DIP

(SERVES FOUR)

1 cup shredded, mild cheese (cheddar, or
Monterey jack)
¼ cup salsa

1. Mix the cheese and salsa in a microwave-safe glass measuring jug
or bowl.
2. Stick it in the microwave oven and
nuke at high power until the cheese
melts—about two minutes, three minutes
tops. Carefully remove and let it cool for
a couple of minutes.
3. Serve as a dip for tortilla chips, pita
chips, chunks of French bread, or
cut-up veggies.

BUILD YOUR OWN TRAIL MIX

Nuts and seeds: peanuts, almonds, sunflower
seeds, hazelnuts, sesame seeds
Dried fruit: raisins, golden raisins, date nuggets,
shredded coconut, banana chips, apple chips,
apricots, dried cranberries, dried cherries
Sweet stuff: chocolate chips, white chocolate
chips, chocolates with a candy shell, butterscotch
chips, peanut butter chips
Salty stuff: pretzels, party mix cereal snack,
sesame sticks, breadsticks, mini cheese crackers
Cereals: any breakfast cereal, granola

*The basics: mix one cup of nuts, one cup of fruit, and
one cup sweet stuff together. Add salty stuff and cereal
to taste, and store in an airtight container. What will you
call yours?*

HOLY GUACAMOLE!

(SERVES TWO)

1 ripe avocado (the dark-skinned Hass ones
are best)
Handful of fresh cilantro leaves, chopped
⅛ red onion, chopped into small dice
1½ tsp freshly squeezed lime juice (lemon
works, too)
Salt and pepper, if you like

*For hot shots only: one pickled jalapeño pepper,
chopped into small dice by an adult*

1) The avocado should give when you
squeeze it. Cut the fruit in half on a
cutting board, and lift out the big seed.
Peel off the skin and put the green stuff
into a mixing bowl. (If some avocado
sticks to the skin, scrape it out with a
spoon and add it to the bowl.)
2) Mash the avocado halves against the
sides of the bowl with a fork until they
are really squished into a chunky paste.
Add the other ingredients and mix with
a fork.
3) Gobble the green goodness down with
carrot sticks, celery, or tortilla chips. Yum!

Ask an adult to help you chop the jalapeño

PIZZAS IN THE OVEN

(SERVES ONE)

1 wholewheat or white pita bread (or an English
muffin or mini-bagel)
A few tablespoons of pizza sauce in a jar
¼ cup shredded mozzarella cheese
Lots of your favorite pizza toppings

1. Heat up the oven to 350 degrees.
2. Toast the pita bread or muffin slightly
in the toaster so it doesn't go soggy.
3. Put the toasted bread on a baking tray
and spoon over some pizza sauce, using
the back of the spoon to spread the
sauce. Sprinkle on the shredded cheese.
4. Raid the refrigerator for all of your
favorite pizza toppings. Pile them on
top of the pita.
5. Using an oven glove, slide the tray into
the oven and cook for about ten
minutes, until the cheese melts.
Remove the tray and enjoy.

Remember to turn off the oven.

Nope, they don't sweat it. They regulate their body temperature by making the blood vessels in their tails expand or contract.

RECYCLE YOUR OLD JEANS INTO A COOL BOOK BAG

A TRUSTY, WELL-WORN PAIR OF FAVORITE JEANS CAN BE AS COMFORTABLE AS AN OLD FRIEND. BUT IF YOU'VE GOT JEANS THAT ARE ON THEIR LAST LEGS, THERE'S NO NEED TO FALL APART AT THE SEAMS. INSTEAD, GIVE THEM A NEW LIFE AS A HANDY BOOK BAG. AFTER ALL, THEY DID A GREAT JOB HAULING YOU AROUND—NOW THEY CAN DO THE SAME FOR YOUR SCHOOLBOOKS.

STUFF YOU NEED

Old pair of jeans. If you don't have any, pick some up from the local second-hand store...that's recycling twice!
Sharp scissors
Needle and thread, or a sewing machine
Old leather belt

WHAT TO DO

1 Zip up and fasten the jeans and turn them inside out. Use the scissors to cut off both jean legs about three inches from the crotch. Jeans fabric is tough stuff—you might need a parent to help you. Set aside the jeans legs.

2 Work one side at a time. Fold the cut edges up, then press the side seams up together so they match up.

3 Using a needle and thread or sewing machine, sew each leg opening closed about an inch from the cut edge. You can trim away the excess denim down to about ½ an inch from the stitching. Repeat on the other side.

4 Now turn the jeans right-side out. Make a handle by threading an old belt through the side belt loops and fastening it off. Add a stack of books, and you're good to go.

GO TO PAGE 135

How many words can you write with just one pencil?

MANHUNT!

WHAT YOU NEED:
LOTS OF FRIENDS (AND FLASHLIGHTS IF YOU'RE PLAYING AT NIGHT)

DECIDE YOUR PLAYING BOUNDARIES AND PICK SOMEONE TO BE THE HUNTER. (IF LOTS OF KIDS ARE PLAYING, YOU MIGHT WANT TO HAVE TWO OR THREE HUNTERS.) THE HUNTER CLOSES HIS EYES AND COUNTS TO A HUNDRED WHILE EVERYONE ELSE SCATTERS.

WHEN THE COUNT IS OVER, THE HUNTER SIGNALS THAT THE MANHUNT HAS BEGUN. HE SEARCHES FOR THE HIDDEN PLAYERS, TAGGING THEM OUT, UNTIL ALL THE PLAYERS HAVE BEEN FOUND. (PLAYERS DON'T HAVE TO STAY IN ONE HIDING PLACE; THEY CAN MOVE AROUND.) THE LAST PLAYER FOUND BECOMES THE HUNTER FOR THE NEXT GAME.

Gotcha!

You will need: lots of kids

Get everyone to sit in a circle with their legs crossed. Ask them to put their heads down as one person chosen as "It" walks around the outside of the circle, eventually tapping one kid on the head. This person is the eliminator. When the "It" kid gives a signal, everyone should raise their heads. **The "It" kid tries to eliminate other players by winking at them, without being spotted by anyone else. If you are winked at, you must count to ten and then play dead. Lie back in the grass. (If you want to add some sound effects or show your acting skills, go ahead!) If "It"** manages to get everyone out, he wins. If you think you spot the eliminator, you can accuse him—if you're right, you win, and you get to do the tapping next round. If you're wrong… uh oh, you're dead.

Want big, brilliant bubbles, without toil or troubles?

HOLD A SOAP-BUBBLE BLOWING CONTEST

Here's how to make the most gigantic soap bubbles ever. You can buy giant bubble wands, but it's fun to make your own and mix up a special bubble potion that will produce streams of enormous rainbow-colored beauties. Try this with your friends, and see who can make the biggest, longest-lasting bubbles.

You won't want to stop until there are none left to pop!

What to get:

- Long (72-inch) shoelace or equivalent length of heavy-duty string
- Two plastic drinking straws
- 12 cups of water
- One cup of good-quality dishwashing liquid
- 3–4 tsp glycerin (you should be able to find this at the drugstore)
- Large bucket

Optional bubble-makers: old metal coat hanger, kitchen funnel, plastic strawberry basket

WHAT TO DO:

1

The day before, mix up the bubble solution. Stir together the water, the dishwashing liquid, and the glycerin in a bucket. Mix slowly so you don't get lots of foaming. Leave overnight.

2

Thread the shoelace (or piece of string) through two plastic drinking straws and tie the ends together to make a large loop.

3

Next, put the loop into the bucket of bubble mixture. Let it soak in, so the shoelace is really saturated with soap.

4

Carefully lift up the shoelace loop, holding a straw in each hand. Slowly swing the frame through the air. To release the bubble, give the straws a little twist in opposite directions. Don't worry if you don't get it right first time, or even the second and third times . . . it takes practice.

5

Why not experiment with other objects? Try dipping the wide end of a funnel into the soapy stuff and blow through the small end. Dip a strawberry basket and zip it through the air. Even a stretched-out old coat hanger can make brilliant bubbles.

RUN THE BEST LEMONADE STAND IN THE ENTIRE WORLD!

LEMONADE AND A SUNNY DAY just belong together. Setting up a lemonade stand is a great way to learn the basics of business. But you don't want to run a standard stand...you want to set up the most stupendous, most superior, most staggeringly great lemonade stand in the whole world. Never fear...start right here.

LOCATION, LOCATION, LOCATION: the three things to keep in mind. (Oh, and a fourth: lemonade.) Pick a public place where people can see you. Choose a spot where lots of people walk or drive by, and can easily stop to sample your wares.

BIG IT UP: make a big sign to advertise your stand. Keep it simple and eye-catching. People in a hurry want to know right away what you are selling. You could also post flyers nearby, but make sure to collect them at the end of the day so you aren't littering.

THE SET UP: make a good-looking stand. A card table is perfect. Cover it with a plastic tablecloth and set a cooler of ice underneath. Add a price list. If you're selling lemonade to raise money for a good cause, let people know! You'll need a box with a lid to hold money (better have a few dollars in change to start off with), and why not set out a tip jar, too? Throw a couple of quarters in...it may encourage your customers to do the same.

METHOD:

1 CUP WATER
1 CUP SUGAR
1 CUP LEMON JUICE (MADE FROM ABOUT 4–6 LEMONS)
4 CUPS COLD WATER
EXTRA LEMON & MINT FOR GARNISH

**FOR SYRUP: COMBINE WATER AND SUGAR IN A SAUCEPAN. BRING TO BOIL, STIRRING UNTIL SUGAR DISSOLVES. LEAVE TO COOL IN REFRIGERATOR.
FOR LEMONADE: MIX THIS SIMPLE SYRUP WITH LEMON JUICE AND COLD WATER OR SODA WATER.**

THE PRODUCT: wash your hands, prepare your lemonade and keep it in an insulated jug so it stays nice and cool. You can also sell other stuff: freezer pops, cookies, watermelon slices, or chilled juice boxes. Oh yeah...sample before you serve, so you know your lemonade is the tastiest in town.

SERVICE WITH A SMILE: Greet every customer. Even though lemons can make you pucker up, be sure to smile as you hand over your lemonade.

1. Get a sponge, a bucket of warm, soapy water, and a couple of old t-shirts or towels. Stand your bike on its kickstand (or lean it on a wall) somewhere where it's OK to splash a little water. Give your bike a once-over. If it's majorly muddy, knock off any big clumps.

2. Use the garden hose to give your bike a light spray, to remove most of the surface dirt. (No hose? A bucket of water will work, too.) Don't soak it—you might wash away some of the lubricants your bike needs to run well.

3. Dip the sponge in the soapy water and start washing the bike frame. Take it easy— rubbing off abrasive mud and dirt can scratch your bike frame.

This is a good time to give your bike a thorough inspection to check for loose or broken parts. Wash off the seat and handlebars, too. Then wash the wheels. Rinse with another blast from the hose.

WHEELIE CLEAN

DOWNLOAD PAGES FROM THIS BOOK, CLIPART, AND OTHER COOL STUFF AT

www.kiddk.com/handbook

ICHTHYOLOGY

FISH   STUDY OF

NOTE:

FISH NOT TO SCALE!

MAROON
CLOWNFISH

CORAL
BEAUTY
FISH

KOI CARP

PYJAMA
CARDINALFISH

NORTHERN PIKE

LONGNOSE
GAR

ARCHERFISH

GOLDFISH

SPOTTED
RAY

SPINY BOXFISH

THREE SPOT
ANGELFISH

CLOWN
TRIGGERFISH

WEEDY
SEA-DRAGON

BLACKTIP REEF
SHARK

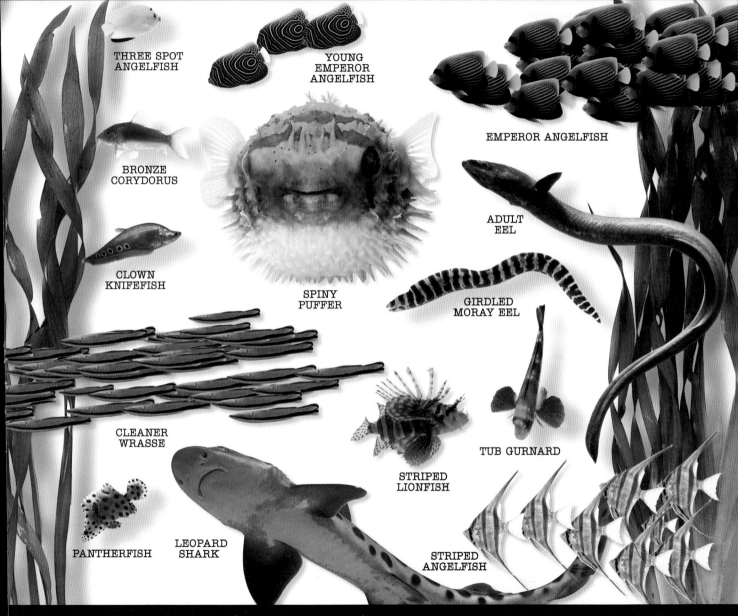

THREE SPOT
ANGELFISH

YOUNG
EMPEROR
ANGELFISH

EMPEROR ANGELFISH

BRONZE
CORYDORUS

ADULT
EEL

CLOWN
KNIFEFISH

SPINY
PUFFER

GIRDLED
MORAY EEL

CLEANER
WRASSE

TUB GURNARD

STRIPED
LIONFISH

PANTHERFISH

LEOPARD
SHARK

STRIPED
ANGELFISH

GIVE THE PLANET A HUG

Do something...not nothing

Buy rechargeable batteries

Unplug your phone charger when not in use

Ride your bike (or take the bus or walk) instead of taking the car when you can

Turn off your computer and room lights when you're not using them

Re-use plastic shopping bags and recycle them when they're worn out

Clear out your room and give the good-quality stuff you don't need to a charity store

Start a compost heap for kitchen waste

Don't leave the DVD player, your computer, or the TV on standby

Use fans instead of cranking up the air con

Buy recycled stuff (like school supplies) when you have the choice

Turn off the faucet when you are brushing your teeth... and smile about the good deed you've just done

REDUCE, RE-USE, RECYCLE!

Don't buy stuff that is wrapped up in excess packaging. Just say no

Set your computer printer to do double-sided printouts (on recycled paper, naturally)

Convince your parents to install energy-efficient light bulbs. Now there's a bright idea

Don't run the dishwasher or washing machine until it's full of dirty stuff

♥ YOUR PLANET

EVERYTHING THERE POSSIBLY COULD BE TO KNOW ABOUT RECYCLING

Any time you find a new use for something old, that's recycling. So, does that mean when you blow up your empty potato chip package and pop it in your sister's ear you are helping to save the planet? Not exactly! Here's how recycling really works, and what role it may play in the future of our planet.

WHEN DID RECYCLING BEGIN?

People have been doing it for thousands of years. Before the industrial revolution, goods weren't cheap to buy or quick to make. People wouldn't dare think of tossing something broken away and buying a new one, like we often do today. So everyone tried to get the longest and the most use out of the stuff they had. In the 1930s, grim economic conditions meant that people had to recycle, as they couldn't afford to buy new things. In the 1940s, many households recycled certain things like metals to help support the war effort. After the war, lots of people forgot about recycling, because the economy was booming.

In the 1960s and 70s, recycling again became an important issue, as people started to become even more smart and aware about the Earth and how we treat it. Recycling is now widely seen by most people as a great idea.

SO WHY RECYCLE?

For a start, it reduces the amount of garbage sent to landfills. Americans dump more than 100 million tons of trash into landfills every year. Not only do these take up a lot of room, the stuff thrown into them (and the yucky chemical soup released when garbage decomposes) creates pollution. Recycling also uses up fewer natural resources, as you aren't starting from scratch when you recycle something. It generally takes up less energy, too, although this is not always true. Recycling can save money and create jobs, too. It's all good, really.

WHAT CAN I RECYCLE?

Almost anything can be recycled. Among the most commonly recycled goods are paper, glass, and steel, which are turned into new paper, glass, and steel. (Imagine this: you hand in your homework, you get it back, you recycle it, and then someday, it comes back to you as a new assignment. Cool!) Aluminum cans can be melted down into new cans. Simple enough. Plastic is tricky because there is so much of it—it's cheap to make—and it does not biodegrade (break down). Recycled plastic is usually made into fabric or construction materials. Lots of companies specialize in recycling other goods, such as e-waste (electronic goods). It takes a lot of work, though, and there are many nasty chemicals that can be released during recycling.

SO WHAT DO I DO?

Contact your local or city government and find out what recycling programs they support. (A cool idea: arrange a school field trip to the recycling center, so you can see how it all works up close.) In many places, recyclable stuff is picked up with the rest of the garbage. Sometimes you have to sort the stuff yourself, and other times it's done for you. There are also drop-off centers for recyclable stuff. Sometimes these give you money for bringing in your goods. Recycling is not cheap, and the more people who participate, the lower the costs will be. The US recycles about 30 percent of its waste, but some European countries (Germany, Sweden, Austria, and the Netherlands) recycle as much as 60 per cent of their stuff. Think about the other things you might recycle. When you put your mind to it, there are lots of old things that can have a new life. You can collect worn clothing, shoes, and bedding, and donate them to a local shelter or charity. A children's center might welcome toys and books. Check the phone book for a list.

Some critics say recycling costs way too much. They don't think there is a garbage problem. Why not take this as a challenge? Write a report to convince people that recycling is essential now and for the future. Maybe your local paper will print your story. Help show that they need to turn their old ideas into new ones...come to think of it, that's recycling.

MAKE SURE YOUR STUFF IS UNBEARABLE (FOR BEARS)...

START ▶

1

REST AREA

TOURIST INFO CENTER

WHEN YOU'RE TRAVELING THROUGH BEAR COUNTRY, it's an extremely good idea to follow some basic precautions to prevent an unwelcome visit from a hungry or curious bear. As anyone who's camped where bears are known to roam will tell you, they are extremely determined once they smell something good to eat. Let's face it, it's one thing for you to hug a teddy bear, but it is another thing entirely for a real live bear to hug you. Follow a few sensible steps to protect your stuff and stay safe, and you might just escape a fate that is beyond unbearable.

2 **IN YOUR CAR,** keep all food items double-bagged in a cooler and lock it in the trunk. Keep trash bags in the trunk, too. This includes everything edible, from a pack of chewing gum to a half-empty soda bottle. (Bears will be drawn by anything that has a scent, so non-food items like soap, baby wipes, or cosmetics will also attract them.) A bear who sniffs out potential grub will have no problem ripping the car door off to get to the food.

DOWNLOAD PAGES FROM THIS BOOK, CLIPART, AND OTHER COOL STUFF AT
↓
www.kiddk.com/handbook

3 WHEN YOU'RE OUT ON THE TRAIL, keep your food nearby and don't leave it for even a moment. Don't invite any bears to your picnic by being careless.

4 DON'T LEAVE FOOD or scented items such as toiletries in your tent, for the same reason. You must store your food in food lockers. If they are not provided, you can usually rent them. Keep your locker closed and latched shut at all times, only getting out the food you are using for each meal.

5 TREAT YOUR TRASH in the same way, locking it away in the food locker or throwing it away in a bear-proof dumpster.

6 IF YOU SPILL SOME FOOD or ketchup on your clothes it's a good idea to change them before you go to bed. You don't want to wake up with the wrong kind of teddy.

7 WASH YOUR DISHES after you eat and clean up any pots and pans. Even if you think a bit of crunchy, overcooked stew is yucky, a bear will find it delish.

FINISH

BE NICE TO YOUR SISTER!

You've probably been hearing this since you were a little kid. But what exactly do you need to do to be nice to the person who is sometimes the most incredibly annoying person in the entire world?

1 Smile! If you smile at someone, it's almost impossible for them not to smile back, and that's a pretty good thing, right?

2 Try to do things together now and then, especially stuff that makes you both laugh.

3 Be a good listener. Let her know that what she has to say is important to you. (This will help her to be more willing to listen to you, too.)

4 If she is really bugging you, take yourself somewhere else. Go for a bike ride, go to your room and read a book, shoot some hoops, whatever. Take your frustration out somewhere else.

5 OK, you're related but it doesn't mean that you agree on absolutely everything. You might not share her taste in music, movies, or friends, but just agree to disagree. Keep an open mind—she might just introduce you to something new and cool that you like.

6 Try to remember that you're family, so you must have some sort of common ground somewhere. Find it, and you'll go a long way toward understanding each other.

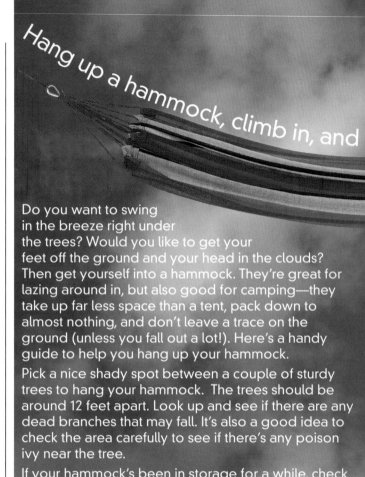

Hang up a hammock, climb in, and

Do you want to swing in the breeze right under the trees? Would you like to get your feet off the ground and your head in the clouds? Then get yourself into a hammock. They're great for lazing around in, but also good for camping—they take up far less space than a tent, pack down to almost nothing, and don't leave a trace on the ground (unless you fall out a lot!). Here's a handy guide to help you hang up your hammock.

Pick a nice shady spot between a couple of sturdy trees to hang your hammock. The trees should be around 12 feet apart. Look up and see if there are any dead branches that may fall. It's also a good idea to check the area carefully to see if there's any poison ivy near the tree.

If your hammock's been in storage for a while, check it out and make sure it is in good condition. You can put it up following the manufacturer's instructions. But if you want to hang it with rope, cut two pieces of ½ inch nylon rope, each about 8 feet long. Fold the rope in half, then put one half of the rope through

relaxxxxxxx

the hammock chair loop. Pick up both ends of the rope, pull them over and then through the loop. Pull tight.

Now put the ends of the rope around the tree and tie them with a loose overhand knot. Check that the hammock is hanging high enough off the ground, then pull the rope to tighten the knot.

Then, pull the ends of the rope to the front again and cross them under the first circle of rope. Make another overhand knot. To finish, pull the ends of the rope to the back and tie two overhand knots. Do the same on the other side.

Here's the fun part: get in! Here's what you do: back up to the hammock, pull the far end up and over your head, and then lie back. Pull your feet in and move around a little until you are comfy. To get out, sit up, put your feet on the ground and stand up. If it's too tricky getting in and out, you might need to alter the height of your hammock.

Be careful. Don't try to stand up or you'll find yourself tipped out.

SLIME

MAKE UP A BATCH OF SILLY SLIME. YOU CAN STRETCH IT AND SNAP IT, AND IT ALWAYS RETURNS TO NORMAL. IN FACT, THE LONGER YOU PLAY WITH IT, THE MORE FUN IT GETS! IT'S A LITTLE BIT MESSY, SO KEEP IT AWAY FROM CLOTHING, FURNITURE, AND CARPETS.

STUFF YOU NEED:

½ cup white school glue
½ cup liquid laundry starch
Mixing bowl and spoon

WHAT TO DO:

Measure glue and liquid starch into a bowl. Stir together thoroughly. Let the mixture rest for five minutes. Then knead it with your hands, until it comes together. It will suddenly turn into a glob of goo that is irresistible to play with. You can keep it fresh in a zip-close bag or in a small jar with a lid.

make a worm farm

Earthworms don't just wriggle...they do a lot of work to improve the soil. Worms munch through decaying plants and animals on the surface of the ground, then as they tunnel down through the soil, they deposit their waste behind them. This action helps to mix up the soil and distribute rich nutrients from the surface. The network of tunnels let the soil breathe and help rainwater drain away, too. You can see this for yourself by setting up a worm farm. Bonus points: it will totally gross out your sister, too!

HOW WORMS WIGGLE

If you study a worm up-close, you will see it is divided into around a hundred, donut-shaped segments—these are muscles. There is also a long muscle that runs right along its body. To move along, the worm contracts the segments and stretches the body muscle forward, as tiny bristles help it to hang on to the soil. Then the worm contracts its long muscle to draw the rest of the body behind the front, so moving along inch by inch.

WHICH END IS WHICH?

Do you know your worm's head from its tail? It's not easy to tell, is it? Here's what to do: put your worm in a dish. Touch one end very carefully with a paintbrush. The worm pulls back. Next, touch the other end and watch it shrink back. The end that shrinks the quickest is the tail. Now say hello to the right end of your wormy pal.

STUFF YOU NEED:

Clean sand

Potting soil

Some fallen leaves and grass cuttings, or veggie scraps (no onions or garlic)

Large glass bowl

Water

Worms

WHAT TO DO: to set up your farm, fill up the bowl with alternating layers of soil and sand. Cover the top with a few dead leaves, grass cuttings, or vegetable scraps from the kitchen. Add enough water to dampen the soil, but not to drench it completely. Pour in a little bit and test it...you can always add more. Then collect a few worms and add them to the bowl. Keep your farm in a cool, dark place. Check out your farm every day. You will be able to see tunnels as the worms eat through the layers, and very soon they will mix up the sand and soil. When you finish observing the worms, put them back where you found them.

WORLD OF WORMS
There are an incredible 2,700 species of worm wriggling around the world. In just one acre of land, there might be a million worms. Worm pee is called tea and worm poo is called castings. One Australian worm, the Gippsland, can grow to 12 feet long. Now, that's one radical wriggler.

ASTOUNDING TRICKS TO CONFOUND YOUR FRIENDS

CAN YOU MAKE THE IMPOSSIBLE POSSIBLE? ARE YOU THE KIND OF KID WHO NEVER TURNS DOWN A CHALLENGE? YOU ARE? BET YOU CAN'T RESIST THESE DARING AND DEVIOUS TRICKS. ALL YOU NEED IS PAPER, A PENCIL, AND SOME SCISSORS. STEP RIGHT UP, AND PREPARE TO AMAZE YOUR FRIENDS AND FAMILY WITH THESE FANTASTIC FEATS AND SPECTACULAR STUNTS.

WALK THROUGH PAPER

CAN YOU CLIMB THROUGH A SHEET OF PAPER?

YES, you can...and here's how to make the cut.

1) Use a regular sheet of printer paper. Fold it in half lengthwise.

2) Now, make horizontal cuts across the paper from alternate sides. Don't go all the way across.

3) Open up the sheet of paper and cut along the vertical fold in the center, leaving the top and bottom rows uncut.

4) Next, open out the paper very carefully. You will be left with a giant ring large enough to climb through with ease.

STEP ON IN, AND YOU HAVE WALKED THROUGH A SHEET OF PAPER.

GO THROUGH A KEYHOLE

OK, you've walked through a single sheet of paper. Can you get through a keyhole? The secret is unlocked here.

1) Bet your friend that he or she cannot go through a keyhole. Unless your friend is really, really, really tiny, the answer will be no.

2) Write your name on a small piece of scrap paper, fold it up, and push it through the keyhole.

CONGRATULATIONS...YOU HAVE JUST GONE
THROUGH A KEYHOLE!

WRITE WITH YOUR NOSE

So far, so amazing. Now tell your friend that you can write with your nose! It's an audacious claim, but you can make it true (unless your friend is starting to smell a rat...)

1) Tell your friend that, yes, you can write with your nose. Hold a sheet of paper (not the same one you walked through!) up and pretend to scribble on it with your nose if you're feeling dramatic. Challenge your friend to top this feat. It's not likely, is it?

2) Then, write, "WITH MY NOSE!" on the sheet of paper and show it to your friend with a flourish. You have written with your nose—and that's nothing to sneeze at.

HOLE-Y AMAZING

ONE SMALL HOLE IN A SHEET OF PAPER, ONE
IMPOSSIBLE CHALLENGE...OR IS IT?

CUT A TINY HOLE in the middle of a sheet of printer paper, smaller than your pinky finger. Now, challenge your friend to push his finger through the hole without tearing the paper.

IT'S NOT GOING TO WORK,
IS IT?

NOW ASSURE YOUR friend that you can put your finger through the center of the paper. Tell him you won't tear a thing. Then, roll the paper into a tube, and push your finger into the center.

YOU'VE DONE IT!

GO TO PAGE 125

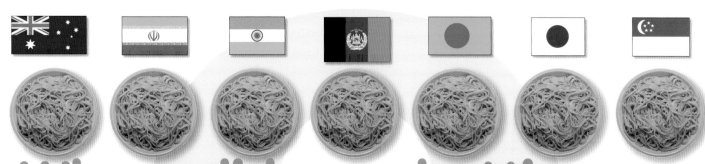

Where did spaghetti come from anyway?

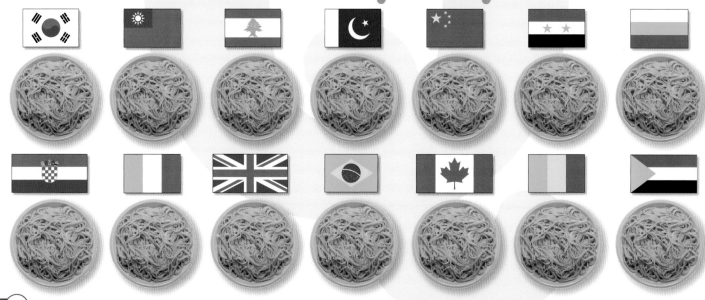

VOLUNTEER!

ARE THERE PLENTY OF HELPING HANDS AMONG YOUR FRIENDS? Can't put your finger on exactly what to do? Why not organize a group volunteer project? Find someone who needs help and have a fun day pitching in together. At the same time, you'll do something for your community that deserves a round of applause. And we've got to hand it to you: donating your time and energy to helping others is worth a big thumbs-up.

Meet with your friends to decide what kind of project you are interested in. Some ideas: neighborhood or park clean-up projects, helping out at the local food bank, collecting clothing for a homeless shelter, working on a holiday toy drive, or volunteering at the local animal shelter. You're bound to have lots more good ideas!

Next, contact a group that connects volunteers with local agencies. Your school teacher should be able to direct you (through the phone book or the Internet) to the right organization. Meet with a representative of the group to offer your help. (Some volunteering opportunities aren't good for kids, so make sure he or she knows the ages of the people in your group.)

When you've agreed a volunteer project, put everything down in an e-mail or handout (date, start and end time, address, and directions to the site, contact people, supplies to bring, any special clothing requirements, etc.). Make sure this email or handout goes to everyone who wants to be involved. Encourage as many people as possible to help out.

On the big day, get to the site a little early so you can say hello, make sure everything is set up, introduce your friends as they arrive, and motivate everyone and have fun!

The **AARDVARK** is a mysterious and solitary creature that is only active at night. Its diet consists almost exclusively of ants and termites, which it consumes in huge numbers. One aardvark's evening meal might consist of an incredible 50,000 insects.

The **ROCK HYRAX**, a small fuzzy mammal, is able to scale vertical walls of rock. There are hundreds of tiny muscles in the soles of its feet that pull the middle into a suction cup that grips tightly, so the hyrax can climb even the steepest surfaces.

FLAMINGOS can only eat with their heads upside down. Like ducks and geese, they filter feed, sucking water through their mouths and straining out food. But flamingos put their beaks in shallow water upside down, and move their heads from side to side. Their tongues act like pumps, sucking water into the front of the bill and pushing it out the sides up to 20 times a minute. Bet you can't do that.

Not all animals have taste buds on their tongues or in their mouths. The **HOUSEFLY**, for example, tastes through its feet. That means it can relish your delicious hamburger as soon as it lands on it! Yuck.

ANIMAL FACTS

The only spot on a **DOG'S** body that contains sweat glands are the pads on its feet. (Dogs also cool down through panting.) On a hot day, a dog's dogs must really be barking!

Despite what our eyes tell us, **POLAR BEARS** aren't white. In fact, their long, coarse guard hairs are actually hollow and colorless. Polar bears only look white because the hollow cores scatter and reflect visible light, in the same way as snow and ice.

The inland **TAIPAN SNAKE**, which slithers around Australia, is the most venomous land-dwelling snake in the world. Each snake has enough venom to kill about 100 people.

The **GIANT ANTEATER** has one of the longest tongues among animals. Its two-foot-long tongue is coated in sticky spit. The anteater flicks it deep into an ant's nest, then slurps in its "catch".

How much water does a **CAMEL** hold in its hump? Absolutely none. Instead, its hump is filled with fat that it can convert to energy when needed. Camels can go for long periods of time without any water, but they can easily gulp down an astounding 13 gallons at a time when they do have a drink.

MALE MOTHS are the top smellers in the animal kingdom. They use their antennae to collect scent particles given off by female moths. Some can detect the scent of a female fluttering more than six miles away.

SWIFTS spend almost their entire lives airborne, night and day. So how do they sleep in flight without crashing into objects or each other? One study showed that they kept aloft through hovering, moving very little and flapping their wings very gently, maintaining a more or less stationary position.

20" Pizza

The deep-sea dwelling **GIANT SQUID** has the largest eyes of any animal, measuring an astounding 20 inches across. That's about the same size as an extra-large pizza!

COOL AREA

www.kiddk.com/handbook

ALLIGATOR ENCOUNTER

MY, what big teeth the crocodilians (**crocodiles**, **alligators**, and **caiman**) have... and you certainly don't want two rows of them wrapped around your leg, do you? Crocs and gators kill hundreds of people a year. While it's unlikely that you will be gobbled up by a gator, do you know what to do if you suddenly find yourself face-to-face with one. See you later, **alligator**!

1 Stay well away from alligator-infested waters. Don't even dare to dip a toe in a river or lake if there are gators around, especially at night, when you can't see as well (but the alligator can see its potential prey just fine, thank you.) Please don't dangle your legs over the edge of a boat, either, if you are at all attached to them.

2 If you do spot a croc, get away. Try to put as much distance as you can between you. They can move surprisingly quickly.

3 In the unlikely event that you can't get away and the gator attacks, fight back. Go for the eyes with a stick or boat oar if you have one handy, or just poke them with your fingers. The nostrils are another vulnerable spot. A sharp smack in the snout might just save your life.

4 If you are bitten and you manage to get away, get medical help right away. An alligator's mouth is full of bacteria (ever seen an alligator brush its teeth? Or floss? Didn't think so.) which can infect your wound.

TRACK ANIMALS

ALL ANIMALS leave behind droppings, also known as **scat**. You can gather a great deal of information from scat, so don't turn your nose up at it (even if some of it is pretty smelly.) An expert can tell the kind and size of animal, when it had its last meal, and what it ate all from checking out its scat. It takes a while to get that scat-smart, but there is plenty you can tell right away. The most important thing to remember: **don't handle animal scat with your bare hands**. Wear thick rubber gloves, and clean them and your hands afterward with antibacterial soap.

WHERE TO LOOK
Some animals tend to leave their droppings in a specific place, known as a latrine. These spots are often smelly, so follow your nose to find one.

WHAT TO LOOK FOR
Study the shape of the scat to find clues about what animal left them behind. **Herbivores** (like deer or rabbits) tend to leave rounded droppings, while carnivore droppings are usually long, and pointed. Take a closer look to see if the droppings contain any indigestible matter. A herbivore's scat might contain bits of plant fiber, while a carnivore's scat can have fur or bits of bone from their prey in it. If the scat is deep in color and moist-looking, they are probably fresh. Old scats are paler and more dried-out.

Rabbit

Duck

Otter

Roe deer

BY THEIR SCATS

WHO DUNNIT?
Here are some common types of scat.
Remember, don't touch!

RAT DROPPINGS
Shaped like grains of rice,
as other rodent scat.

FOX DROPPINGS
Tube-shaped scat with pointed
end. Racoons and skunks leave
droppings of a similar shape.

RABBIT DROPPINGS:
Small, dark brown spheres,
usually found in clumps.

WILD CAT DROPPINGS
A thin, rounded tube that
may be partially buried. Like
domestic cats, wild cats often
dig holes for their droppings.

DEER DROPPINGS:
Dark, round, and plentiful—deer
eat a lot of vegetation so they
leave plenty of scat behind.

OWL PELLETS
These may look like droppings,
but they are not. Birds don't
have teeth to chew up their
food, so they may swallow it
whole. Then, they regurgitate
the indigestible bits as a ball
called a pellet. If you are lucky
enough to find one (try an old
barn or around the bottom of a
tree where owls roost) you can
moisten it with a little water,
then pull it apart to find the tiny
bones and animal fur within.

A coughed-up pellet from an owl

Little owl pellet

Short-eared owl pellet

Songbird pellet

Barn owl pellet

THE MOST TWISTED

If Stu chews shoes, should Stu choose the shoes he chews?

SIX THICK THISTLE STICKS. SIX THICK THISTLES STICK.

Peter Piper picked a peck of pickled peppers.
Did Peter Piper pick a peck of pickled peppers?
If Peter Piper picked a peck of pickled peppers,
where's the peck of pickled peppers Peter Piper picked?

**Top chopstick
shops stock
top chopsticks.**

ALICE ASKS FOR AXES. Sam's

shop
stocks
WHICH WRISTWATCHES ARE SWISS WRISTWATCHES?
short
spotted

She sells seashells on the sea shore.

The shells she sells are surely seashells.

So if she sells shells on the seashore,

I'm sure she sells seashore shells.

A skunk sat on a stump and thunk the stump stunk, but the stump thunk the skunk stunk.

socks.

102

Cinnamon aluminum linoleum.

TONGUE-TWISTERS EVER COLLECTED

A big black bug bit a big black bear, made the big black bear bleed blood.

THE SIXTH SICK SHEIK'S SIXTH SHEEP'S SICK.

How much wood would a woodchuck chuck
if a woodchuck could chuck wood?
He would chuck, he would, as much as he could,
and chuck as much wood as a woodchuck would
if a woodchuck could chuck wood.

THREE FREE THROWS.

Ike ships ice chips in ice chips ships.

chop shops stock chops.

If two witches were watching two watches, which witch would watch which watch?

Big Ben blew big blue bubbles.

103

WHO SEES SEASHELLS BY THE SEASHORE?

Nothing beats the beach. Surfing, swimming, sand castles, sun...and studying? While the beach is an excellent spot to hang out and have fun, it is also a perfect place for studying nature because it is home to so many living things. Here are some cool ways to explore and enjoy the seashore and find out about the plants and animals that live there.

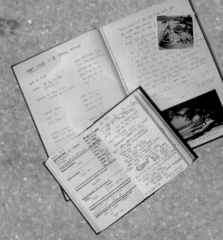

SEASHELL COLLECTING

At the beach, look for empty shells on the sand, on rocks, and in shallow pools. Pick the best of each type and put them in a bag or sand bucket. (A mesh bag is good, as the excess sand shakes out.) Remember, only collect empty shells, with no living animals still inside. When you get home, wash the shells in cold water to remove all the sand and seaweed, then leave them to dry on paper towels. You could make a display case for your shell collection, using a seashore guidebook or the Internet to help you identify the shells and the creatures that once made them their homes.

SEAGLASS AND SEA STONE COLLECTING

You can also comb the beach for sea glass: beautiful fragments tumbled smooth by the sand and the waves. Try to collect as many colors as you can. Green, brown, and amber fragments are fairly easy to find, while blue, purple, and red sea glass are rare treasures. You can also start a collection of the unique stones that wash ashore. You might focus on a particular color or shape of stone, or you might look for rocks that have been marked with a unique pattern. Depending on where you are, you may al be lucky enough to find sand dollars, ammonites, or even semi-precious stones. If you like, you can use a marker pen to write the date and location.

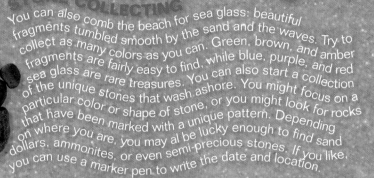

BEACH JOURNAL

Create a diary to describe the plants and animals you encounter at the shore. (A pair of binoculars will come in handy for spotting birds and far-away animals.) Make drawings and take photos to illustrate your journal, and stick in bits of shell, feathers, fur, plants, and any other items you comb from the beach. Take notes about when and where you saw animals, and what they were up to. When you're dune...or, done, you will have an excellent record of your beachcombing days.

BE CREATIVE

SEASIDE SCULPTURES

Sandcastles are cool, but why not think bigger, and create a giant sculpture in the sand? Maybe you will make a pirate ship, or a giant squid, or even a life-sized shark. You need lots of wet sand, so plan your creation near the water's edge (but make sure the tide is not on its way in.) Push the sand into shape and smooth it down with your hands, then use tools like pieces of driftwood or sticks to carve details into your work of art. You can decorate your super sculpture with pebbles, strands of seaweed, twigs, or other items you find on the beach.

MINIATURE SAILING FLEET

Make a collection of tiny sailing ships with stuff you find on or near the beach. Sticks, hollow rushes, thin shells, or bits of driftwood make excellent boats. You can lash together a handful of sticks with some seaweed or plant stalks to make a raft. Ferns and big leaves can turn into sails. Keep your ships to display, or launch your mini-ships into the sea.

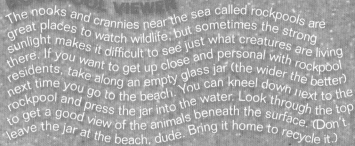

ROCKPOOL VIEWER

The nooks and crannies near the sea called rockpools are great places to watch wildlife, but sometimes the strong sunlight makes it difficult to see just what creatures are living there. If you want to get up close and personal with rockpool residents, take along an empty glass jar (the wider the better) next time you go to the beach. You can kneel down next to the rockpool and press the jar into the water. Look through the top to get a good view of the animals beneath the surface. (Don't leave the jar at the beach, dude. Bring it home to recycle it.)

HEY, YOU! **Want to put a little spring in your step? Jumping rope is a fun way to get fit. It's not strictly playground stuff...boxers and other athletes train with a jump rope. To get started, you'll need to find the correct size jump rope. If it's too short, you might trip yourself up. Too long, and you'll never get swinging. Hold one end of the rope in each hand, and stand with both feet in the middle. The ends of the rope should reach your armpits. (If you've got a little extra, you can tie knots in the rope near the handles to make it shorter.) Are you ready? Jump to it!**

BASIC JUMP

1. Wear some good jumping shoes. Hold the ends of the rope in both hands, with your elbows tucked into your body and arms bent. Put your thumbs on top of the handles.

2. Start with the rope behind your heels and swing it over your head. Just as the rope gets to your toes, jump high enough to clear it. Bounce lightly on the balls of your feet, with knees relaxed and slightly bent and feet together. Land on both feet, and don't jump too high! If you're jumping to get fit, you want to build up your stamina by increasing the length of time you can jump a little at a time. Try to pick up a little speed when you get the hang of it.

THE TRICKY STUFF...

Side swing

Hold the rope with both hands together and swing it to your right, hitting the ground, then to your left, hitting the ground again. Then jump as normal. Keep alternating the right and left swings with jumps.

Twister

On the first swing of the rope, twist your hips to the right as you jump. Keep your shoulders facing forward. On the next jump, twist your hips to the left, then the right, and so on.

Can-can

Jump on your left foot, lifting up your right knee. On the next swing of the rope, jump with your feet together as normal. Now jump on your left foot, and kick your right knee in front of your body. Next, jump with your feet together again to finish the sequence. Repeat with your left leg.

COOL TRICKS TO DO WITH A JUMP ROPE

RAKE A BIG PILE OF LEAVES...AND JUMP IN!

Colorful autumn leaves are beautiful in the trees, but not so pretty when they are scattered over the yard. Raking up the leaves not only makes the yard look neater, it's also an essential chore. Leaving layers of leaves around can smother the grass so it doesn't grow well in the spring. Pick a fine, dry day to rake up leaves. It will be much easier to rake them if they have dried out a little in the autumn sun. Once you've raked a pile of leaves together, it will be almost impossible to resist jumping in. Go ahead. Okay, it makes a little more work, but it's a blast.

- The first thing to think about is what you're going to do with all those leaves! Are you going to load them into a wheelbarrow and roll them off to the compost pile, or bag them up in special leaf bags? Find out if your town has special rules for getting rid of leaves.
- Get your equipment together: a rake, leaf bags, gloves to stop your hands from blistering, and maybe a wheelbarrow. Take a bottle of water, too.
- You won't be able to tackle the whole yard in a day. The best plan is to rake a little bit at a time.
- Start raking the leaves into several piles. Keep your back straight and your arms steady as you pull the leaves toward you. Switch sides from left to right every so often, so you work your muscles evenly.
- Take a break every hour. This is tough work!
- When you've made a pile of leaves that is big enough, go ahead and jump in if you like.
- Load the piles of leaves into bags or the wheelbarrow so you can dispose of them properly.
- Do you have a neighbor who is unable to do yard work? Why not pitch in with your friends, and offer to rake up their leaves for them? The more people who pitch in, the faster you will finish. Don't leaf anyone out of the fun.

Could you really fry an egg on the sidewalk on a hot day?

Whittle a Walking Stick

A trusty walking stick is a handy hiking tool (and a great gift for an outdoorsy person.)

- When you're hiking in a wooded area, keep an eye out for a branch that is the right length to use for a walking stick.
- Look for fallen branches that aren't too old and dried out, so they still have strength and flexibility. The ideal branch will be slightly thicker at one end—for a handle.
- When you've found a contender, start to whittle the bark off the branch with your pocket knife.
- Remember the safety rules—work to the side and away from your body. When the bark is removed, smooth off the end of the handle into a slight dome shape, and level off the thinner end until it is flat.
  - You can carve your own name into the stick, or if you are giving it as a gift, carve that person's name. Finish the stick off with a rubbing of linseed oil buffed into the wood to make it shine.

BANISH A BUG FROM YOUR HOUSE

BE A HOUSEHOLD HERO AND GET RID OF THE SUPER-SCARY, EIGHT-LEGGED SPIDER THAT IS CREEPING YOUR SISTER OUT, ONCE AND FOR ALL. DON'T STEP ON IT, THOUGH. CATCH IT, PACK IT UP TO GO, AND CARRY IT RIGHT OUT OF THE DOOR. GIVE THAT BUG A BRAND-NEW START IN A NEW LOCATION.

YOU NEED A PLASTIC CUP AND A THIN SQUARE OF CARDBOARD LARGE ENOUGH TO COVER THE CUP (OR A SHEET OF PAPER FOLDED IN QUARTERS). A CLEAR CUP IS BEST SO YOU CAN SEE WHAT IS (OR ISN'T) INSIDE. COVER UP THE BUG WITH THE CUP.

NEXT, CUT OFF ITS ESCAPE ROUTE. HOLDING THE CUP SECURELY, LIFT ONE EDGE A TEENY BIT AND SLIDE THE CARDBOARD UNDERNEATH. GET UNDER THE ENTIRE MOUTH OF THE CUP.

NOW LIFT UP THE CUP, HOLDING ON TO THE CARDBOARD. TURN IT RIGHT-SIDE UP SO YOU FREE UP ONE HAND. OPEN THE DOOR AND GO OUTSIDE, THEN CROUCH DOWN AND RELEASE THE CAPTIVE. MAKE SURE YOU SEE IT GO OUT OF THE CUP...YOU DON'T WANT TO BRING IT BACK HOME WITH YOU. THEN GO BACK INSIDE, AND WAIT FOR YOUR SISTER TO THANK YOU.

The whole world is yours to explore...from city streets to the deep forest, mountaintops to riverbeds, sandy shore to rocky outcrops. Hiking is a brilliant way to see the world, and get some good exercise, too. You will make your heart and lungs stronger and work your muscles, while all the while opening your eyes to the beauty around you. All you need to make your move is your own two feet, some advance planning, and lots of initiative. (A good pair of socks is also a plus!)

TAKE A HIKE!

PLANNING YOUR HIKE

Before you even think about lacing up your hiking books, make a trip plan. Ask yourself the following questions to help you prepare and focus:

- **Where will you go on your hike?**
- **When will you be back?**
- **Who is hiking with you?**
- **What are you taking along?**
- **Why are you going?**

FEET FIRST

You don't want to put a foot wrong out on the trail, so you need good footgear. If you are good to your feet, they will take you almost anywhere.

SHOES OR BOOTS

When the going is easy, almost any pair of shoes is fine for hiking. If the terrain is tougher, or the weather more changeable, hiking boots are a good choice. Ones with leather uppers will support your feet and ankles best, and protect your feet from the elements. Boots with fabric uppers are fine for hiking in good weather. Whichever shoes you choose, they should fit well, be worn in, and sturdy.

It's a good idea to bring along another pair of shoes— old sneakers or sandals are perfect—to

wear around camp on an overnight hike, so you can air out your hiking boots and knock a little bit of the mud off them.

Hiking socks made of wool or a wool/synthetic mix help keep your toes cozy and draw sweat away from your feet. Many hikers wear a thin pair of socks underneath the outer pair to reduce the chance of getting blisters, but make sure your boots or shoes have enough wiggle room before you try this. Cotton socks are fine for short hikes, but when they get wet, they stay wet. Take some extra socks. If you're getting weary, changing into a fresh pair of socks can make you feel much better.

WHAT TO WEAR

Layer your clothes so you are prepared for any weather conditions, as the temperature can suddenly change. A T-shirt is a great first layer. Long pants and long-sleeved shirts are good for keeping bugs and sun out and protecting you from scratchy thorns and brush. Cargo pants are great for hiking because the pockets come in really handy. A lightweight fleece jacket won't add much bulk but will keep you toasty should the weather change unexpectedly. If you expect rain (or even if you don't) pack a light waterproof jacket or rain poncho. A baseball cap or a brimmed hat can shade you from the sun. Throw in a couple of bandannas and you're good to go.

PLAN

- Where will you go on your hike? Mark up a copy of your proposed route on a map, and leave it behind, especially if you will be hiking in a remote area.
- When will you be back? Make an action plan, in case you do not return at the specified time.
- Who is hiking with you? Make a list of everyone's name and contact information.
- What are you taking along? Use this as a checklist to help you pack your gear.
- Why are you going, and what challenges do you think you may face and overcome?

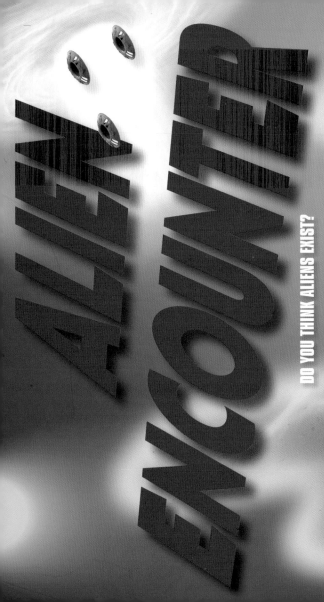

ALIEN
ENCOUNTER

DO YOU THINK ALIENS EXIST?

If they are real, do you imagine they are keeping their multiple bugged-out eyes on you?

ARE THEIR SILENT SPACESHIPS SET ON A DIRECT COURSE TO YOUR BACKYARD?

Do their foul fifteen-fingered hands reach out for you as you sleep so snugly and blissfully unaware in your bed?

DO THEY HAVE A PICTURE OF YOU ON THEIR REFRIGERATOR?
COULD YOU SURVIVE AN ALIEN ENCOUNTER?

LOOK OUT...
LOOK OUT...
IT'S BEHIND YOU!

DON'T BE AN EASY TARGET FOR AN ALIEN ENCOUNTER. IF YOU HAVE THAT FEELING SOMEONE IS WATCHING YOU, THEY PROBABLY ARE. BE EXTRA AWARE AND EXTREMELY CAUTIOUS. THERE ARE MANY SIGNS THAT THE ALIENS HAVE YOU UNDER SURVEILLANCE. IF YOUR PET ACTS STRANGELY, BARKING OR MEOWING AT SOMETHING THAT ISN'T THERE, THEY MAY BE WARNING YOU ABOUT AN ALIEN'S PRESENCE. OTHER SIGNS MIGHT INCLUDE FREQUENT COMPUTER CRASHES, LOST HOMEWORK, MISSING SOCKS, AND AN UNTIDY ROOM THAT HAS CERTAINLY BEEN RANSACKED BY CURIOUS BEINGS FROM ANOTHER WORLD. AT LEAST, THAT'S WHAT YOU CAN TELL YOUR MOM.

IF AN ALIEN HAS YOU IN ITS SIGHTS, IT WILL TRY EVERY TRICK IN THE ALIEN HANDBOOK TO CONTROL YOU. ALMOST ALL ALIENS ARE CAPABLE OF SHOOTING OUT HIDEOUS PARALYSIS RAYS FROM THE FRONTAL LOBES OF THEIR BRAINS, THAT STOP YOU FROM MOVING AWAY AND GETTING OUT OF THEIR VILE CLUTCHES. IF YOU FEEL THIS IS HAPPENING, GRAB YOUR GAMES CONTROLLER OR TV REMOTE, AIM IT IN THE DIRECTION OF THE ALIEN (GUESS), AND START PRESSING BUTTONS UNTIL YOU JAM THEIR RAYS.

ALIENS ALSO LIKE TO TRY MIND-MELDING TRICKS TO GAIN CONTROL OF YOUR VERY BRAIN. A VERY GOOD WAY TO PREVENT THIS IS TO EAT LOTS OF ICE CREAM OR ICY SMOOTHIES IN REALLY HOT WEATHER, SO THAT YOU GET THE BRAIN-FREEZE SENSATION. THEIR FOUL TRICKS ARE USELESS AGAINST A FROZEN BRAIN. IN THE WINTERTIME, STICK YOUR HEADPHONES ON AND PLAY AN ANNOYING POP SONG OVER AND OVER TO HELP PROTECT YOUR BRAIN.

IF NOTHING SEEMS TO WORK, AND THE ALIEN IS INTENT ON WHISKING YOU AWAY TO ITS HOME PLANET SO THAT YOU CAN BECOME SOME KIND OF SINISTER SCIENCE PROJECT, TELL THEM THAT YOU HAVE LIBRARY BOOKS DUE AND THAT YOU CANNOT POSSIBLY LEAVE TOWN WITHOUT RETURNING THEM. THEN GRAB SOME BOOKS AND PRETEND YOU ARE GOING TO THE LIBRARY. GET ON YOUR BIKE AND PEDAL AS FAST AS YOU CAN!

One of the major dangers mountaineers face is an avalanche, a huge, mega-devastating slide of snow or rock down a mountainside that can engulf everything it its path. An avalanche moves with incredible speed and power, causing massive destruction to anything in its way. Let's hope that doesn't include you. Here's what you need to know in case you are ever caught up in an avalanche.

1) Forget about all your equipment (like your snowboard or skis and poles.) Leave it and worry about yourself.

2) The avalanche is likely to pick you up and sweep you along, so assess the terrain around you. Hopefully you are not near a cliff's edge or surrounded by large trees. If there is any shelter (behind a rocky outcrop or a building, for example) find it, get down low to the ground, and turn away from the avalanche. Cover your nose and mouth with one hand, while you brace yourself with your other hand. Don't scream…you'll end up with a mouthful of avalanche.

Avala

nche!

3) As the force of the avalanche surrounds you, your goals are to make air space around your face and to try and get to the surface. Wave your hand in front of your face to make an air pocket. Use kicking motions to propel your body through the snow. Survivors describe it as "swimming" the avalanche, which has got to be a whole lot better than sinking.

4) When the avalanche stops, try to dig your way to the top. If you can punch an arm or even a leg through the snow, you will have a much greater chance of being spotted and rescued. Time is not on your side; keep as calm as you possibly can, and use your head.

DO A GOOD DEED TODAY

KINDNESS IS CONTAGIOUS

Make cookies for the family next door

HELP AN ANIMAL IN TROUBLE

PLAY WITH A CAT AND A PIECE OF STRING

Shoot some hoops with your mom

Take out the garbage

Show your respect for nature without being asked to

Ask your sister if she needs help with her homework

WRITE AN E-MAIL TO GRANDMA

Give directions to someone who's lost

VOLUNTEER FOR SOMETHING

Organize a classroom clean-up day

PICK UP BANANA PEELS BEFORE SOMEONE SLIPS

Teach your brother how to play chess

CLEAN YOUR ROOM **Plant a tree**

Surprise someone

Send grandpa a text message

Read a story to the little kids in the neighborhood

Pick up trash at the local park

Offer to help before someone asks

116

Do frogs have ears?

Fearsome predators fully equipped with terrifying jaws of doom, sharks are incredibly scary killing machines. Fortunately, they attack people very rarely. But "rarely" is not the same thing as "never", so here's what to do if you are unlucky enough to find yourself face-to-face with an extremely kid-unfriendly shark. Yikes.

SHARK ATTACK

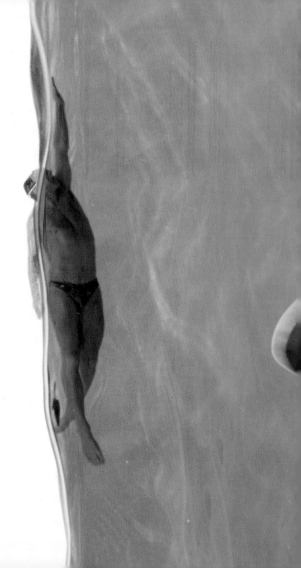

1) OBVIOUS, but true: the best way to prevent a shark attack is to stay away from them. Way, far away. IF YOU SEE A SHARK IN THE WATER, DON'T GO IN.

2) AVOID SWIMMING WHERE SHARKS HAVE BEEN SEEN. There will be signs posted on the beach if sharks have been spotted in the area. Please don't ignore them. If you are swimming in an area where sharks have been known to pay a visit, swim in a group instead of alone, AND DON'T SWIM AT NIGHT.

3) IN THE UNLIKELY EVENT THAT A SHARK DOES SPOT YOU, TRY YOUR BEST TO STAY CALM AND SWIM AWAY AS QUICKLY AS YOU CAN. GET BACK TO THE SHORE, WHERE YOU WILL BE SAFE.

4) IF THE SHARK DOES ATTACK, try to hit it on the nose with your fist, your surfboard, an oar—whatever works. The shark just may back off, long enough for you to swim to shore. If it manages to bite you, be aggressive. POKE IT IN THE EYE WITH YOUR THUMBS OR HIT THE SHARK HARD ON ITS GILL OPENINGS. DON'T PLAY DEAD. FIGHT BACK WITH EVERYTHING YOU'VE (STILL!) GOT.

5) IF YOU HAVE BEEN BITTEN, and you get away, get out of the water as fast as you can. Any bleeding might draw the shark back for a second, probably deadly attack. Get medical help AS QUICKLY AS YOU CAN.

TO CATCH FISH, YOU GO FISHING. To catch the school bus, you go to the bus stop. To catch a cold, you inhale someone else's germs. But exactly how do you catch a snake? What should you do if you spot a snake in your garden, and want to get rid of it without hurting it? First of all, make sure it isn't venomous. Check a field guide or use the Internet to be positively sure of what kind of snake you are dealing with. If you are in doubt, phone the local animal shelter or pest removal department and let them handle things. If the snake is definitely not venomous, try shooing it away with a stick, a broom, or some other object. If the snake absolutely won't budge, here's what to do.

HOW TO CATCH A SNAKE

Get a stick and hold it in front of the snake to distract it from you, as you stand slightly to one side. The idea is, to get the snake to focus on the stick and not on you. You want its head pointing away from you before you attempt to grab it.

Quickly grasp the snake by its neck. You'll need to get your fingers close to its head, so it can't turn around and bite your hand. Don't squeeze so hard that you kill it, but be firm. You can grab the tail with your other hand to stop if from wrapping around your arm.

Now carry the snake out of your yard, far enough that it doesn't decide to slither right back. Face its head away from you and quickly let go of it. Then get out of there. Wash your hands thoroughly after touching a reptile, as they can carry the Salmonella bacteria.

What if someone's pet snake escapes inside the house?

Get a pillowcase, and an old t-shirt or towel. Find the snake. Sit the pillowcase nearby, crumpled down like a discarded sock. Throw the t-shirt over the snake's head. It will probably be scared enough to coil up under the t-shirt. Right away, scoop the shirt and the snake into the pillowcase and bundle the ends together. Put the snake back in its tank.

CAUTION!
BEWARE OF
POISONOUS
SNAKES

Over a lifetime, the average person will dream some 130,000 dreams in all. If you put it all together, that's a stupendous six solid years of dreaming. (There is no study to find out how many of those dreams are about monsters.)

CRYSTALS

In chemistry and mineralogy, a crystal is defined as a solid substance consisting of a regularly repeating arrangement of atoms, ions, or molecules.

Blue topaz

Brown topaz

Almandine

Unrefined chrysoprase

Clear calcite

Stilbite crystals on quartz

Galena

Polished rock crystal

Crystal with carnelian

Brazilianite crystals

Dolomite crystal

Sinhalite crystal

Culprite crystal

Smoky quartz

Strontianite

Unpolished topaz

Chrysoberyl

Aquamarine (Beryl)

Ruby crystal

Rose quartz crystals

Mass of pyramid-shaped amethyst

Diamond crystal

Rhodochrosite

Flos Ferri Aragonite

Rhodochrosite on stone

Nitratine

Pink translucent calcite

Five aquamarines

Silicon dioxide (quartz)

Cerussite

Calcite trigonal crystal

Green fluorite

Peridot

Cut sapphire

Zircon crystal

Rhodochrosite on stone

Prismatic crystal

Cleaved fluorite crystal

SAY HELLO TO THE WORLD!

Albanian Tung

Arabic Al salaam

Botswana Dumella

Cajun Bon jour

Chinese Ni hao

Czech Nazdar

Finnish Päivää

French Bonjour

German Guten Tag

Greek Kalimera

Hebrew Shalom

Hungarian Szia

Hindi Nah-mah-STAY

Indonesian Selamat pagi

Irish Dia Dhuit

Italian Buon giorno

Japanese Konichiwa

Korean Annyong ha shimnikka

Maori Kia ora

Norwegian God dag

Polish Czesc

Portuguese Bom Dia

Punjabi Sat Sri Akal

Russian Zdravstvuite

Serbo-Croatian Dobar dan

Slovenian Sivjo

Spanish Hola

Swahili Jambo

Swedish God dag

Tagalog Magandang napon

Taiwanese Ii ho

Thai Sa-wa dee

Tibetan Tashi Delek

Turkish Merhaba

Urdu Assalam-o-alaikum

Welsh Bore da

A team of archaeologists in China recently uncovered an incredibly well-preserved bowl of 4,000-year-old noodles made from ground millet seeds. These Neolithic noodles are the oldest examples of spaghetti (pasta) ever found. Italian explorer Marco Polo probably brought pasta to Italy after his travels to Asia.

SKELETON

Bone up on the real names of your internal skeleton. These are all based on Latin.

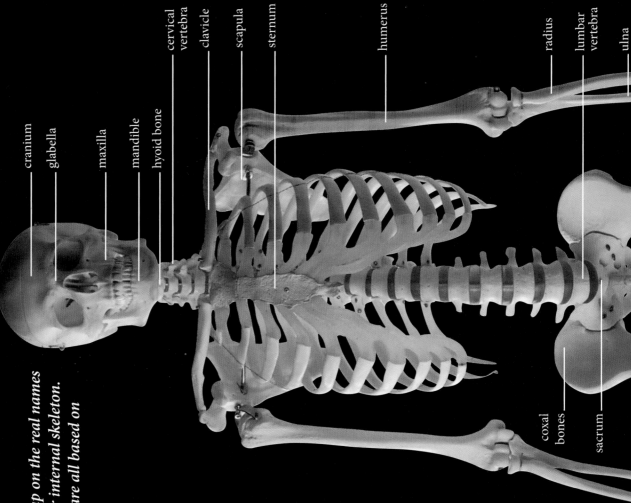

cranium

glabella

maxilla

mandible

hyoid bone

cervical vertebra

clavicle

scapula

sternum

humerus

radius

lumbar vertebra

ulna

coxal bones

sacrum

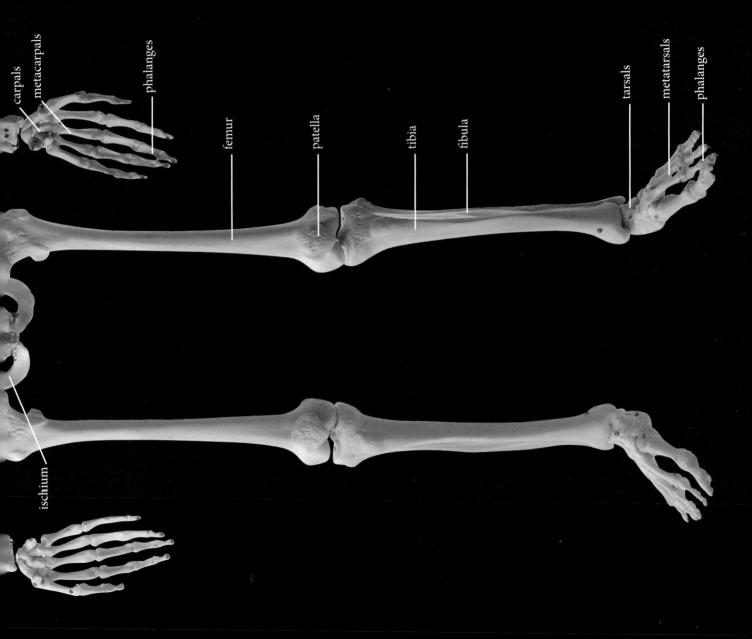

carpals

metacarpals

phalanges

femur

patella

tibia

fibula

tarsals

metatarsals

phalanges

ischium

ENTOMOLOGY

insects | study of

There are over a million different species of insect and this makes them some of the most successful critters on Earth.

Red Spotted Longhorn Beetle

Pierrot butterfly

Jewel wasp

Frog beetle

stag beetle

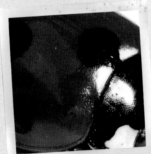
Ladybug

Minotaur beetle

Black beetle

Minotaur

American cockroach

Termite

House Fly

Leaf beetle

Red giraffe weevil

Schulze's agrias
butterfly,

Bumble bee

Glasswing

praying mantis,

(side view)

soldier termite

Dung beetle

Ant

Dragonfly

wasp

Surinam cockroach

Get out the family photo albums and share them around. Give awards for the geekiest clothes, the cheesiest grin, the worst haircut, the sweetest smile, the cutest pet picture, the most unflattering photo, the nicest vacation memory, and more.

Start a family journal. Everyone is welcome to add to it.

Plan a family building or decorating project and make sure everyone pitches in.

Have a family slumber party. Sleep in the living room and stay up late.

GO FOR A FAMILY BIKE RIDE OR NATURE HIKE. PACK A PICNIC TO TAKE WITH YOU.

Create a family portrait gallery: draw pictures of each other.

Sing loudly in the car. You could even make it a talent contest. Who has lots of talent and who has almost none?

Get some language learning CDs from the library, and learn to speak a foreign language together. Try to make it through one dinnertime speaking the new language.

HAVE A MOVIE NIGHT. POP PLENTY OF POPCORN, AND WATCH A MOVIE TOGETHER. THE YOUNGEST ONE PICKS ONE WEEK, THEN THE NEXT YOUNGEST, AND SO ON.

Go bowling together, play a round of miniature golf, take a spin at the go-karting track, or visit the local batting cages.

Write a story together.

Dig out all the old board games and have a game night. You might also want to play your family's favorite card game—or learn a new one.

GO FOR A NICE LONG WALK. TREAT EVERYONE TO ICE CREAM CONES AFTERWARD.

Pretend there's a power cut. Turn off computers and the television, light some candles, and tell stories.

MAKE A FAMILY COOKBOOK. ASK ALL YOUR RELATIVES TO ADD THEIR FAVORITE RECIPES.

131

HOW TALL IS

Trees are the tallest and longest-living plants in the world. Say you want to figure out exactly how tall a tree is, and how many birthdays it has had. No, you don't need a massive measuring tape, and you

HOW TALL IS IT?

You'll need a pencil, and a friend who knows how tall he is. Ask your friend to stand at the base of the tree.

Stand far enough away from the tree so you can see the whole tree without moving your head up and down. Hold a pencil in your hand and stretch your arm out, so that your elbow is locked. Then, line up the tip of the pencil with your friend's head. Put your thumb on the pencil to line up with your friend's feet. (Do his socks match, by the way?) The bit of the pencil you are holding now represents the scaled height of your friend. See how many pencil lengths it takes to reach the top of the tree, then do the math. If the person standing next to the tree is five feet tall, and it takes six pencil lengths to get to the tree top, then the tree is about 30 feet tall.

THAT TREE?

don't need an ax to cut down the tree so you can count its growth rings. Instead, get a regular measuring tape, a pencil, and a friend to help you find the answers.

HOW OLD IS IT?

Here is a quick and easy way to guess the age of most trees. It works because many common trees grow a similar amount each year. Use the measuring tape to measure the distance around its trunk (the circumference) in inches at a point about five feet from the ground. Then divide this number by 1 in, to get the approximate age of the tree in years.

MAKE A BIRD BUFFET

WANT to invite some birds into your backyard so you can take them under your wing and study their behavior? One of the nicest ways to welcome some new feathered friends into your life is setting out a bird feeder.

SO WHY not go to town and set up a bird bistro with loads of different things? In the winter, when there are few bugs and seeds around, birds will be extremely grateful. In summer, they will still to stop by in search of a snack. Add a birdbath for them to splash around in, and your backyard may be the top of every bird's to-do list.

STUFF YOU NEED

Birdseed	Unshelled peanuts Other mixed nuts Peanut butter Pinenuts	Oats Leftover rice Stale bread Crackers Cereal
Shortening Rolling pin and plastic bag Mixing bowl and spoon Measuring cup Paper plate	Table knife Plastic cup or empty yogurt tub, to mold bird pudding Two or three large pinecones Milk carton or large cardboard juice container	Large sewing needle and thread Garden twine Twigs

What's on the menu?

NUTS ON A STRING

Cut a length of string about 24 inches long, thread one end through a sewing needle, and tie a large knot in the other end. Then, take a handful of unshelled peanuts and pierce them with the needle to thread them on to the string. Be careful...the needle is sharp. Hang the nutty necklace up on a tree branch. Birds will go nuts for them. You can also make strings of other nuts, such as walnut halves or pecans, or try a mix of all kinds of nuts on one string.

PEANUT-Y PINECONES

Cover the bottom of a paper plate with 2 cups of birdseed. Then pick up a pinecone and slather it with peanut butter. Get right into the nooks and crannies. When the pinecone is extremely peanut-y, roll it in the birdseed, really pressing it in, and set aside. Coat the additional pinecones in the same way, then hang them up in a tree with garden twine.

BIRD PUDDING

Gather up some kitchen scraps in a large mixing bowl. Put stale cereal, crackers, or bread into a plastic bag, seal the top, and crush into crumbs with a rolling pin, then add to the mixing bowl. You can sprinkle in birdseed or nuts if you like. Ask an adult to melt some shortening (enough to bind the scraps together into a paste), carefully add it to the bowl, and stir it until you have a stiff paste. Pack the pudding into plastic cups or empty yogurt tubs. Place a twig in the middle of the mix, and stick it in the fridge to harden. When it is set, tip it out of the mold and tie the twig to a tree branch with garden twine. (You can also stuff the bird pudding mix into the crevices of a pine cone.)

There's enough graphite (a form of carbon) in a single pencil to draw a line about 35 miles long, or write about 45,000 words!

A DOZEN DANDY THINGS TO DO WITH A BANDANNA

First aid: In an emergency, you can use a bandanna as a sling or tourniquet.

Cushion: Lay two bandannas down flat on top of each other. With a sewing needle and embroidery floss, stitch around three sides. Stitch the final side together, but stop about two thirds of the way along, so there is a gap. Turn the cushion inside out, fold it up, and put it in your pocket. When you need a soft place to sit on the trail, you can fill it up with leaves or grass, then empty it out when you are ready to move on.

Headband: fold the bandanna into a triangle, then, starting with the long end, fold it over and over until you get to the point. Wrap around your head and tie.

Sunny-day cover-up: spread the bandanna out and make an overhand knot in each corner. Put it on your head and adjust the knots to fit. Now the sun won't sizzle your scalp.

Bandanna trick: How do you tie a knot in a bandanna without letting go of the ends? Impossible? Here's how. Fold your arms, grab the ends, slowly unfold your arms, so tying a knot, and hey presto! Your bandanna is tied.

Instant air-conditioning: When the temperature soars, soak a bandanna in ice water, wring it out, then plop it on your noggin. That will give you a cool head!

Make a parachute: cut four lengths of string and tie to each corner of the bandanna. Attach the ends of the string together and add a small weight, such as a ball of modeling clay. Drop it and watch it slowly fall to the ground.

Hiker's hat: fold the bandanna into a triangle, then put the long side along your forehead at the hairline. Bring the two points together behind your ears and tie them with a square knot. Tuck the remaining point under the knot.

Bless you: a bandanna is an excellent handkerchief.

Mind your mealtime manners: a bandanna makes a handy napkin when you're camping.

Neckerchief: fold the bandanna into a triangle and tie the ends around your neck. You can make the knot in the back (like a cowboy) or the front (like a chef).

Dust buster: tie a bandanna over your nose and mouth in dusty conditions.

LEAVE NO TRACE

THE EARTH'S WILD PLACES ARE WONDERFUL. YOU CAN LOSE YOURSELF IN THE WILDERNESS (NOT LITERALLY) AND SOMETIMES YOU CAN IMAGINE THAT YOU ARE THE FIRST PERSON TO EVER DISCOVER A PARTICULAR FOREST GLADE OR RIVER BEND. WHAT A ROTTEN SURPRISE, THEN, TO STUMBLE ACROSS A DISCARDED SODA CAN, A CANDY-BAR WRAPPER, OR SOME OTHER REMINDER THAT SOMEONE ELSE HAS BEEN HERE. IN ORDER TO HELP REDUCE OUR IMPACT ON THE LAND, A GROUP OF NATURE LOVERS SET OUT GUIDELINES FOR HIKERS AND CAMPERS TO FOLLOW, TO HELP THEM TO BE RESPONSIBLE WHEN IN THE WILD. FOLLOW THESE TIPS, AND MOTHER NATURE WILL SMILE AT YOU.

When you are hiking on a trail, stay on it. If you take shortcuts, you can trample and damage the grass and plants, as well as the many micro-organisms living right under your hiking boots, as you pass by. Pick a durable spot (dry grass, rock, or gravel) to set up camp, too.

Leave beauty spots untouched for others to enjoy. One of the most amazing things about exploring nature is the feeling of discovery, so take care to preserve what you find and see.

Remember to leave the stuff you find in the wild, in the wild, as nature intended.

Set up and clean up your campfire properly. Use a fire ring or a grill if it is provided at the campsite.

Be considerate with your trash. Pack it up until you find a designated place to dispose of it. You might not want to carry your used leftover food around, but you've got to accept the challenge and leave nature as you found it.

Remember to use water resources wisely. Don't take a soapy bath in a lake or stream, or wash your camping gear there. Soap can damage the ecosystem.

Respect your neighbors—animals and fellow nature-lovers alike. Watch wild animals from afar—don't get too close, move too suddenly, or make loud noises. You're in their home, so you should follow their rules. Be considerate of other human visitors and respect their privacy.

DID YOU EVER SPEND A LAZY AFTERNOON LYING IN A GRASSY SPOT, AND TELLING EACH OTHER ABOUT WHAT SHAPES YOU SAW IN THE CLOUDS? YOU WEREN'T SIMPLY PASSING THE TIME, YOU WERE LEARNING! YES, REALLY. STUDYING THE WAY CLOUDS APPEAR AND WATCHING THEM MOVE CAN ACTUALLY GIVE YOU CLUES ABOUT WHAT KIND OF WEATHER IS AHEAD. HOW COOL IS THAT?

KNOW YOUR CLOUDS

HIGH-LEVEL clouds are found at altitudes of 20,000–46,000 feet, near the top of the troposphere (that's the layer of the atmosphere that is closest to the Earth, where all the weather happens). Their names all come from the Latin word, cirrus, which means a curl of hair. Check out some of these wispy, icy clouds and you'll see that the name fits. There are three main kinds of high-level clouds (and one impostor!).

Cirrus: pure white, wispy clouds that are blown into feathery shapes by the chilly winds. Watch the direction they move in, and you'll get an idea which way the wind is blowing.

Cirrocumulus: a pattern of tiny, rippling puffs of water droplets that spread out to cover a large patch of sky.

Cirrostratus: a hazy, continuous sheet of clouds that can indicate a change in the weather.

Contrails: the trails of icy water vapor left behind by passing jets are known as contrails. These start out as thin lines but spread out as the vapor disperses, so they resemble cirrus clouds. But they're not.

WHAT IS A CLOUD ANYWAY?

Here's the science: when the sun heats up a wet place on Earth, the water molecules evaporate and begin to rise into the air. As they reach colder temperatures in the upper atmosphere, they cool down, slow down, and eventually stick together in a mass of microscopic water droplets or even ice cyrstals. This process is called condensation. When you've got enough water droplets or ice crystals clinging to each other up there, you've got a cloud.

GET YOUR HEAD

MEDIUM-LEVEL clouds are found at altitudes of 6,500-20,000 feet. The three main types are altocumulus, altostratus, and nimbostratus. These bluish-gray clouds are full of water and can often signal the arrival of rain or snow. So, pack your rain gear when you see them in the sky.

Altostratus: a shapeless sheet of clouds that cover the sky like a gloomy blanket, often producing drizzle or light snow showers.

LOW-LEVEL clouds form near the Earth's surface and rise up to 6,500 feet. They appear to be bluish gray, and contain plenty of water. If these clouds gather together, rain is on the way. Types of cloud include cumulus, stratocumulus, and cumulonimbus. Fog and mist are also included in this group of clouds.

Cumulonimbus: these are biggest clouds of all, this huge piled-up cloud may rise up through all the levels in the shape of a gigantic anvil. The cloud's thin tip points in the direction the weather is moving... handy!

Altocumulus: fuzzy puffs lined up in parallel rows, they resemble cirrocumulus clouds, but are darker and denser.

Nimbostratus: a thick, dark layer of gray clouds that blocks out the sun and can bring heavy rains or snow.

Cumulus: puffy, fluffy white clouds that drift across blue skies, with flattened bottoms and cottony tops.

Stratocumulus: lumpy sheets of low-level clouds that appear to be very thick.

Fog: a thick, extremely wet cloud that forms when warm, wet air moves over the colder ground. Mist and fog are essentially the same thing, but fog is thicker. So, if you can't see anything, get a foghorn!

IN THE CLOUDS

GO TO PAGE 175

If I do my homework every night, will my brain get bigger?

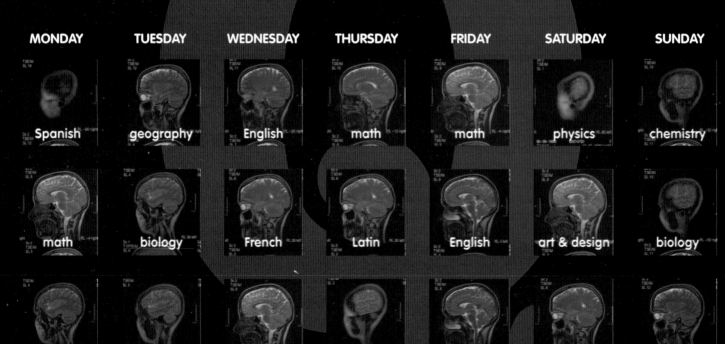

MONDAY	TUESDAY	WEDNESDAY	THURSDAY	FRIDAY	SATURDAY	SUNDAY
Spanish	geography	English	math	math	physics	chemistry
math	biology	French	Latin	English	art & design	biology
math	history	Spanish	art	German	history	math

How to build an amazing campfire

The campfire: it snaps, it crackles, it sizzles, and it lights up the night. A fire is mesmerizing to watch, but you've got to watch out! Fires can be dangerous and extremely difficult to control. So don't even think about lighting a campfire unless you are with an adult who will take responsibility, and unless you have checked the campsite rules to see what is permitted. It goes without saying that you must never leave a fire unattended, and that you must have plenty of water and a bucket of dirt nearby to douse the fire if it gets out of control. So, there is lots to learn before you burn.

Gather up a few handfuls of dried grass, pine needles or pinecones; a few bundles of dry twigs of all sizes; a few handfuls of sticks, a few armloads of logs of all sizes; bucket of water and bucket of dirt to keep on hand, just in case.

Make a ball of dried grass and put it in the middle of the fire pit. Set up a bunch of twigs around it like a tepee. Make a larger tepee on top of the smaller one, with slightly larger sticks. Then make an even larger tepee around the inner layers with small logs, about the size of your forearm.

Ask the adult to light a match and ignite the dried grass. The fire should burn from the inside out. Give it time and give it your patience. Sometimes you have to coax it to burn. Blow on the flames a little to ignite them, if need be. Add more little twigs if you need to, until the fire has really caught. Then ask the adult to put some bigger logs around the fire, still in the tepee shape. Add more logs as the fire burns, if you want to keep it burning. If you want it to burn out, let it do so, then pour water over it and stir the ashes with a stick to make sure they are out. (When you leave the campsite, douse the fire pit with plenty of water again, to ensure no embers still burn.)

NEVER LEAVE A FIRE UNATTENDED

If I sneeze with my eyes open, will my eyeballs pop out?

Bugs, bugs, bugs

They're everywhere. Scientists have named about a million species of insect and there may be many millions more not yet discovered. (Not all bugs are insects, though. To be an insect, you need six legs and a body divided into three parts. That means centipedes don't qualify.) If you want to study the bugs in your own backyard, here's how to catch them for observation, day and night.

DAY SHIFT: pick a damp, warm place and dig a small hole. Put the yogurt tub (or whatever you are using) inside it. Then add a little bit of bug bait: cheese, fruit, a sugar cube, or some cookie crumbs. Cover the jar with a scrap of wood, set the pebbles on top. Leave your trap for a few hours, then come back and have a look. Got bugs?

NIGHT SHIFT: cut the grapefruit in half and scoop out the insides (yummy for breakfast, by the way.) Turn the grapefruit halves upside down and put them in two different spots in your backyard, in the evening. Next morning, turn them over and see who's been visiting.

STUFF YOU NEED:
Old yogurt tub; glass jar or margarine tub
Something to dig with
Bug bait

Four pebbles, roughly the same size
Small scrap of wood
Grapefruit

MAKE BRILLIANT BUG TRAPS!

PACK IT UP!
ALL THE STUFF YOU NEED FOR CAMPING

WHEN YOU'RE PLANNING A CAMPING TRIP (WHETHER YOU'RE GOING ACROSS THE COUNTRY TO A NATIONAL PARK OR JUST ACROSS THE STREET) **THERE'S PLENTY TO KNOW BEFORE YOU GO**. WHERE ARE YOU GOING EXACTLY? WHAT IS THE WEATHER LIKE? WHAT IS THE TERRAIN LIKE? DO YOU HAVE TO CARRY ALL THE STUFF YOU NEED? IS THERE ANY SPECIAL EQUIPMENT YOU NEED? HOW LONG WILL YOU BE CAMPING? SO MANY QUESTIONS, BUT **YOU'LL NEED TO HAVE THE ANSWERS** BEFORE YOU PACK UP A SINGLE PAIR OF UNDERWEAR. . .

GIMME SHELTER!

Tent: you'll need a tent that's big enough for everyone who'll be sleeping inside. To make the rain go away, your tent should be waterproof, and netting will help keep the bugs out. Check the tent over before you pack it up to make sure it's in good repair, that you have everything you need to pitch the tent, and that the zippers are working. (A small rip in the tent can be repaired with duct tape. How handy is that?)

Tarp: this is a sheet of waterproof plastic, or fabric backed with plastic. Spread one underneath your tent to keep the tent floor nice and dry.

Sleeping bags: bundle up at night with the right sleeping bag. You can buy bags in a wide range of prices, sizes, and styles, from simple rectangular bags to mummy bags that keep you snug head to toe. If you will be camping a lot it is worth it to invest in a good-quality bag. Sleeping bags may be filled with down, cotton, or synthetic fibers (which are best for wet weather, as they dry faster.) Some fillings keep you warm in the cold, and others are better for warmer weather. Do a little research on the Internet before you shop, so you make the best choice.

Sleeping pad: even when you're in the great outdoors, it's nice to have a soft bed. A roll-up foam pad or inflatable bed can provide a cushy night's sleep, and keep you off the cold, hard ground, too.

Backpack: you'll need a pack to stow your stuff in. If you are going to do a lot of hiking, take a smaller day pack, too, big enough for a water bottle, sunscreen, and a few extra clothes.

Bags: Stuff several zip-seal plastic bags in various sizes (from sandwich size to gallon-sized) into your backpack. They'll come in incredibly handy for keeping wet clothing separate, holding garbage until you can dispose of it properly, carrying snacks, and more.

Flashlight or portable lantern: they don't call them the "deep, dark woods" for nothing. Get a flashlight so you can see where you're going, and remember to bring some extra batteries, too.

PACK IT UP!
ALL THE STUFF YOU NEED FOR CAMPING

Make a checklist of everything you need for your outdoor kitchen. You can't exactly pack everything but the kitchen sink, now, can you? But you do need to bring along a few culinary essentials including enough food to keep everyone happy. The most important thing to remember: don't go anywhere without a bag of marshmallows.

Camp stove: these portable stoves are easy to use and super-convenient when cooking over an open fire isn't practical or possible. They also leave no trace behind, unlike campfires.

GIMME GRUB!

All you need is a level cooking surface, fuel in the form of small cans called cartridges (ask an adult to handle these), and an appetite. They come in a range of sizes from small backpacker's stoves to larger, multi-burner ones. Follow the directions carefully as improper use is dangerous, and never use a stove without an adult's permission.

Pots and pans: pack a couple of different sizes with lids, so you can cook more than one dish at a time. Choose nesting pans to save space, and lightweight ones are a lot easier to lug around. For breakfast,

bring foods like bacon and eggs or pancake. Bring a frying pan or skillet.

Cook's utensils: pack a few wooden spoons, a measuring cup and spoon set, a plastic cutting board, a pocketknife or multipurpose kitchen knife, a spatula, and some tongs. A nest of lightweight bowls with lids can double as mixing bowls or food storage containers. A couple of kitchen towels will come in handy for drying dishes, and oven mitts will protect your hands when you lift the lid on hot pots.

Cooler: keep things chilled in an ice-packed cooler. You'll need to repack the ice each day, so coolers won't be practical for many camping trips. Carrying a cooler loaded with food can feel like dragging a refrigerator around, so think carefully about taking one.

Dishes and cutlery: each person needs a plate, a bowl, a cup or mug, a knife, a fork, and a spoon. with a marker pen, write everyone's name on the back of the dishes, and initial the cutlery.

Waterproof safety matches: you won't be able to start a fire without them. Never light matches without adult permission. Keep them dry in a zip-seal bag or small, lidded container, as damp matches are no use at all.

Roll of aluminum foil: you won't believe how handy foil is for cooking outdoors. Wrap up food and seasonings in a foil package so the steam can't get out, put the package on the grill rack, and you'll soon be enjoying a delicious dinner (with no dishes to wash up...you can eat right out of the foil if you're careful). You can also use foil to wrap up leftovers. Make sure to collect the foil and bring it home to recycle.

Food and water: whether it's the good fresh air, the hiking, or the teamwork, camping makes you hungry (and thirsty!).You'll need three meals and snacks every day for everyone camping with you. Plan menus for every

day, and make a shopping list. Decide what you can make in advance, and what you will cook on site. Make sure to bring along some salt, pepper, and spices for seasoning. You'll need about a gallon of clean water per person, per day, for drinking, cooking, and cleaning. If your campsite has drinking water (sometimes marked as "potable" water) you're in luck. Otherwise you will need to pack water purification tablets and a water filter to strain out and kill any pesky bugs in water you find. (Boiling water at a full, rolling boil for five minutes will kill most, but not all, organisms.) Make sure you know how to use both the tablets and the filter...you don't want to swallow anything that will make you sick.

PACK IT UP!
NEED FOR CAMPING

GIMME A BREAK

(A CLEAN-UP BREAK AND A BATHROOM BREAK)!

A smelly, grubby camper is not a happy camper. A camper who is desperate for the toilet when none is near is also not a happy camper. You want to be a happy camper, right? (That's why you're reading this book, isn't it?) Here's how to take care of number one (and number two) when you're camping. If your campsite has toilets, sinks, and showers, you're sitting pretty, and you can skip this.

Personal care kit: carry a bar of biodegradable soap or soap/shampoo combination, a washcloth, a small towel, a toothbrush, dental floss, and toothpaste. You'll also need sunscreen, bug repellant, and lip balm. Don't forget toilet paper. To save space, choose a bar of soap or tube of toothpaste that is almost used up. Pack all the dry stuff in one zip-seal bag and the wet, squishy stuff in another. Always wash your hands before eating or preparing food. To clean your whole body up, fill a bowl with water and take it off site. Stay a good distance from lakes, rivers, or streams, even with biodegradable soap. Use the water to brush your teeth and wash up, then scatter the waste water.

Portable shower: here's a cool way to make the dirt go away. Fill up a couple of large zip-seal bag with clean water and leave it in the sun for a couple of hours to warm up. When they are ready, grab your biodegradable soap and find a spot well away from any water source. Hold the bag above your head, poke the bottom of the bag in a few places with a pencil or sharp stick, and enjoy your shower.

Dig a pit toilet: when you've got to go, you've got to go. And if there is nowhere to go, you'll have do dig a hole. Pick a private spot at least 200 feet (about 75 steps) away from any water source. Use a trowel or shovel (or even a thick stick) to dig a hole about six inches deep. Leave the soil you remove piled up alongside the hole. Take your toilet paper to the pit toilet and answer that call! Put used paper in a bag to throw away and kick a little soil from the pile into the pit Make sure the pit toilet is completely filled in with soil when you leave—please.

Yes, they do...right behind their eyes! They don't stick out like our ears do. Instead, they are round patches in the skin that vibrate when they pick up sound, just like our eardrums.

Ribbit!

ear here

TEN THINGS TO DO IN A TENT WHEN IT'S RAINING CATS AND DOGS OUTSIDE

TURN THE LANTERNS OUT AND TELL STORIES. MAKE THEM AS EXCITING, SCARY, AND ADVENTURE-FILLED AS POSSIBLE. WHEN YOU'RE TELLING A GHOST STORY AND WANT TO LOOK SUPER-SCARY, TURN ON A FLASHLIGHT AND PUT IT UNDER YOUR CHIN.

Make shadow puppets (see page 32). It's a hands-down winner.

Crack open a brand-new deck of playing cards and play some classic card games.

MAKE UP A STORY TOGETHER. START WITH ONE PERSON TELLING A COUPLE OF SENTENCES, THEN LET THE NEXT PERSON TAKE OVER. ADD AS MANY CRAZY CHARACTERS AND PLOT TWISTS AS YOU CAN THINK OF.

Tell some dumb jokes (see page 26). Make up some silly

knock-knock

jokes of your own.

WRITE OR SKETCH IN YOUR NATURE JOURNAL. WHAT HAVE YOU SEEN AND EXPLORED TODAY (BESIDES MUD PUDDLES)?

Did anyone bring a harmonica or a guitar?

Challenge everyone to a **Paper, Rock, Scissors** (*see page 155*) **Marathon,** *or try a pencil-and-paper game like* **Hangman, Battleship, or Tic-Tac-Toe.**

Play **CHARADES, I SPY, 20 QUESTIONS,** or another game that you used to play on long car journeys.

PRETEND YOU ARE WRITING A POSTCARD TO YOURSELF AT HOME. WHAT HAS BEEN THE COOLEST THING ABOUT YOUR TRIP SO FAR? WHICH MOMENT WOULD YOU RATHER FORGET? WHAT HAS BEEN THE TOUGHEST CHALLENGE?

WHAT'S THE BEST PET TO GET?

REwARD

✱✱ otto ✱✱

Dogs: there are so many breeds, sizes, and temperaments of dog that you're sure to find a good fit for your family. Popular breeds that are good with kids include retrievers, beagles, Yorkshire terriers, and German shepherds. Many dogs are extremely social and make great playmates. But they do need daily exercise, and larger dogs need outside space. Some breeds need lots of grooming.

CHOOSING THE RIGHT FOUR-LEGGED addition to the family can be a hairy task. How much time can you spend looking after your new furry (or finny or scaly) friend?

Do you live in an apartment or a house with a big backyard? Are there allergies to consider? Have you had a pet before, or is this the first time? Here are some pros and cons for different pets, to help you find one that's perfect for your family.

HOME NEEDED

FOR FUN-LOVING AFFECTIONATE CAT

NAME: pogo
AGE: 2
TYPE: English long hair.
LIKES: sleeping and eating
DISLIKES: being photographed.
NOTE: Pogo has issues.

Cats: feline friends don't take up a lot of space, usually get the exercise they need through playtime, and are relatively easy to care for, although some need more grooming than others. Cats are also known for their independent natures and may not socialize very much (although breeds like the Maine coon and Siamese are usually very social and affectionate.)

'Find Gordon Big Reward

Lizards and snakes: these animals live in tanks, don't take up lots of space, and generally don't require special equipment. Some eat live mice, which might put people off, but others thrive on plants or crickets. Your sister might freak out if a pet snake slithers out of its tank and into her laundry basket, though.

help find home for NIBBLES

mr Nibbles

Hamsters or guinea pigs: both of these are friendly, easy-to-care-for pets ideal for small spaces. Hamsters are nocturnal so they might keep you up at night if they sleep in your room. Neither pet lives for more than two to five years, so may not be good choices for families with younger kids.

STEVE THE TORTOISE NEEDS LOVING HOME

Tortoises: are easy to care for, and long-lived. A tortoise is a cool pet, and is slow-moving, so you aren't going to have to chase it around the house.

missinG

Much loved yellow puffed up porcupine fish BIG REWARD

bruce

Fish: if you don't mind not holding or touching your pets, fish are ideal. An aquarium can be as simple as a fishbowl or as fancy as a saltwater tank. Fish are relatively easy to take care of and you can build a cool world for them to live in with plants and rocks.

ALEX THE RABBIT NEEDS A HOME CAN YOU HELP

Rabbits: a rabbit cage doesn't take up a lot of space, and rabbits are generally affectionate and easy to care for. (You can also train them to use a litter box.) Rabbits do need room to run around when they are out of their cages.

Of course not. Plus, it's virtually impossible to keep your eyes open when you sneeze. Your eyelids snap shut automatically.

HOW TO PLAY A BLADE OF GRASS

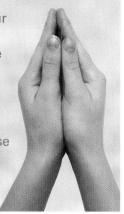

Look for a long blade of grass, about a couple of inches longer than your thumbs, and about a quarter of an inch wide.

Put your palms together, and put your thumbs side-by-side. They should be touching up by the thumbnails and down at the bottom, with a narrow gap in between.

Hold the grass between your thumbs so that it sits in the middle of the gap. The only part of the grass you should be able to see is the edge.

Pucker up as if you are about to whistle. Put your lips over the gap, very close to the blade of grass.

Now blow gently—can you feel the grass vibrate?—gradually blowing harder until you hear a loud squeaky shriek-y sound. **Who knew grass was so noisy?**

PAPER, ROCK, SCISSORS

THE RULES

Three choices, two players, and one simple game you can play anywhere, anytime, this is also a great way to decide who goes first when you're taking turns. Who wants to play Paper, Rock, Scissors?

Players count out loud to three (or say, "Paper! Rock! Scissors!"), each time lifting a closed fist and swinging it down on the count. On the third count, players change their hands into one of three gestures:

SCISSORS CUT PAPER: SCISSORS WIN

Scissors: index and middle fingers stretched out like the blades of scissors

Paper: an open hand

If both players choose the same shape, it's a tie. Play again. You can play best of three games, best of five, or best of a hundred...if you have a lot of time on your hands!

PAPER COVERS ROCK: PAPER WINS

ROCK SMASHES SCISSORS: ROCK WINS

Rock: a closed fist

Hot-diggety Dogs

THE BEST BURGERS AND THE MOST DELISH DOGS

A COOKOUT WOULDN'T BE THE SAME WITHOUT A STACK OF MOUTHWATERING HAMBURGERS AND A ROW OF SIZZLING HOT DOGS, WITH ALL THE TRIMMINGS. HERE ARE A FEW TIPS TO HELP BANISH BORING BURGERS, AND TEACH THOSE OLD DOGS SOME NEW TRICKS. YOUR GRILLING WILL EARN YOU THE TITLE OF CHAMPION COOKOUT CHEF. REMEMBER, YOU'LL NEED AN ADULT'S HELP TO SET UP THE GRILL AND GET IT GOING.

HOT-DIGGETY DOGS

(SERVES FOUR)

4-6 hot dogs (or veggie dogs)
The same number of hot dog buns, split and buttered
A collection of your favorite hot dog condiments: ketchup, mustard (brown and yellow), pickles, relish, sauerkraut, hot peppers, cheese, bacon bits, chopped onion, canned chili, hot sauce, and anything else you can dream up.

1 Prepare all the condiments and set them out on a serving tray. Ask an adult to help light the grill.

2 When it's ready, slap on those dogs. It will take about ten minutes to grill them to perfection. Turn them around a couple of times so they cook evenly. If you like grill marks, leave then on their sides for two minutes.

3 When they are plump and browned slightly, put them aside. Toast the buttered buns on the grill for less than a minute, then serve everything up. Hot dog, you're good!

HAMBURGER HEAVEN

(SERVES FOUR)

1 lb of best-quality ground sirloin, round, or chuck
1 clove of garlic, peeled and chopped (if you like it. Leave it out if you don't.)
Salt and pepper
Hamburger buns, lightly buttered

Yummy toppers: cheese slices, washed and dried lettuce leaves, thick slices of tomato, grilled or raw onion, pickle slices--anything you can think of

Loads of condiments: ketchup, mustard, mayo, relish, barbeque sauce, jalapeño peppers, hot sauce, whatever

1 Get the burger toppers ready and put all the condiments on a serving tray. Wash your hands and tip the ground beef into a bowl with the garlic (if using). Mix it all up. Pull off about a quarter of the meat, form it into a flat ball without squeezing and flatten the ball into a patty. Repeat to make four patties. Season with a little salt and pepper. (Then wash your hands again.)

2 Ask an adult to fire up the grill. When it's ready, put on the burgers and season them again. Grill them for about 7–10 minutes per side. Don't flip them over and over or poke them too much, as the yummy juices might drain out and leave them dry.

3 When the time is almost up, ask an adult to help you check that the burgers are done. Set them aside (not on the same plate as the the one you used for uncooked burgers...raw and cooked meats should never mix) and cover with foil or a pot lid, then slap the buttered buns on the grill. It will take less than a minute. Serve the buns alongside the burgers, with all the fixings. Enjoy!

PS Don't eat meat? Veggie burgers from a package taste great on the grill, too. Check the package directions. Veggie burgers might dry out faster, so you might want to brush on a little butter or oil to keep them moist.

GOOEY **TOASTED MARSHMALLOWS, CRISP ON THE OUTSIDE AND MELTED ON THE INSIDE. YUM. CREAMY, WARM CHOCOLATE. EVEN MORE YUM. ADD A PAIR OF CRUNCHY SWEET GRAHAM CRACKERS. SQUISH ALL THAT YUMMY STUFF TOGETHER, AND YOU, MY FRIEND HAVE YOURSELF A S'MORE, THE CLASSIC CAMPFIRE SWEET TREAT. THINK YOU CAN FIGURE OUT HOW S'MORES GOT THEIR NAME? FORGET ABOUT IT, DON'T THINK, JUST EAT. AND THEN HAVE ANOTHER.**

BASIC S'MORES

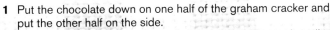

You need:
Half a single-serving milk-chocolate bar
One graham cracker, broken in half
A marshmallow
A perfect marshmallow-roasting stick and a campfire
(The usual stuff about grown-up supervision applies here…)

1 Put the chocolate down on one half of the graham cracker and put the other half on the side.
2 Put the marshmallow on the end of the stick and toast it until it's just the way you like it, from barely golden to nearly burnt. It's your call. About three to five minutes should take care of it.
3 Now use another stick or a fork to slide the toasted marshmallow off the toasting stick, right on top of the chocolate, which will melt a little. Place the graham cracker "lid" on top and squish it down. Let it cool off a little and enjoy. Then make s'more.
(Get the name now?)

CUSTOM-BUILD YOUR VERY OWN S'MORES

Why mess with perfection? Because it tastes so good! Here are some S'mores variations to experiment with. Why not think up your own creative culinary campfire concoction?

Instead of graham crackers: shortbread cookies, coconut cookies, gingersnaps, chocolate-chip cookies, fudge-covered cookies, peanut butter cookies, cinnamon graham crackers
Instead of milk chocolate: dark chocolate, peanut butter cups, butterscotch chips, chocolate thin mints, white chocolate, candy-covered chocolates
Add-ons: peanut butter and jelly, pineapple, apple, or strawberry slices, fruit jam, chocolate syrup or other ice-cream toppings, sprinkles, mini-chocolate chips, crushed malted-milk balls, salted peanuts, granola cereal

S'mores galore!

GO TO PAGE 167

What is the world's largest flower?

If you are lucky enough to have a weeping willow tree in your backyard that needs a haircut, you can create this simple summer shelter from the clippings. You'll need an adult to help you cut the willow branches and stems, and tie the top of the wigwam. Once the basic shelter is finished, you can decorate it with leaves, twigs, and other natural stuff. You'll have your own cool place to hide out all summer long.

What you need:
- A dozen sturdy willow branches, about 6 feet long
- 25-30 lighter willow branches for weaving
- Strong garden twine and scissors
- String
- Two tent pegs or short sticks, for measuring

1 Clear a grassy, level area for your wigwam and make sure your parents are OK with your building plans. You don't want them to wig out, do you?

2 Cut a length of string about 3 feet. Tie it between two tent pegs or stubby sticks. You'll use this to mark out the wigwam's circumference. Stick one peg in the center of the area you've cleared, pull the other peg out in a straight line until the string is taut, then push it into the ground to make a mark. Make a circle of 12 evenly spaced holes. This is where the uprights will go.

3 Push the uprights into the ground, angling them slightly so they meet at the center. Ask an adult to tie them together at the top with garden twine.

4 Now you can begin weaving the lighter willow branches in and out of the uprights to create the wigwam walls. Leave a space so you can crawl in and out. You can use more branches if you want more substantial walls, or keep your wigwam open and airy. Decorate with extra twigs, long grasses, leaves, flowers, or pinecones, or weave in scraps of colored cloth if you like, to make your wigwam one of a kind.

COOL AREA
↓
www.kiddk.com/handbook

WAY-COOL WILLOW WIGWAM

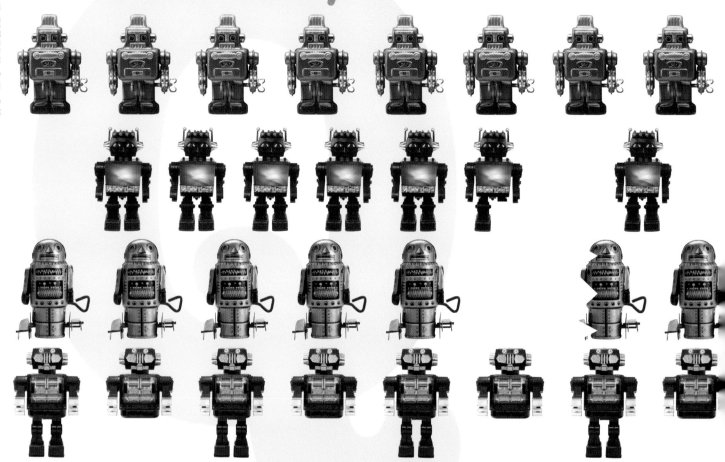

GO TO PAGE 181

Are there really robots on Mars?

INCREDIBLE NUMBERS

10 A googol is a number represented by 1 followed by 100 zeroes.

,000,000,000,000,000,000,000,000 ,000,000,000,000,000,000,000,000,000,0 00,000,000,000,000,000,000,000,000 ,000,000,000,000,000,000

2,000,000,000 Hello? There are more than 2 billion cell phones in use worldwide.

1,500,000,000 There are about 1.5 billion cows in the world, a quarter of them in India.

600,000,000 There are more than 600 million PCs in use worldwide.

100,000,000 Around 100 million text messages are sent every day.

29,017 The height of Mt. Everest, without snow or ice, is 29,017 feet.

2,297 When it is completed in 2008, the Burj Dubai will be the tallest building in the world. It is expected to soar some 2,297 feet above Dubai in the United Arab Emirates, shattering a number of skyscraper records.

6,000 There are more than 6,000 "living" (actively spoken) languages in the world.

900 There are more than 900 different kinds of bat in the world.

400 Germany is the country with the most zoos. There are around 400 there.

292 There are 292 ways to make change for a dollar, using pennies, nickels, dimes, quarters, and fifty cent pieces.

102 102 is the smallest number with three different digits.

71 The sea covers approximately 71 percent of the Earth's surface, and contains 97 percent of all its water.

20 20 per cent of the world's population lives in China.

18 About a third of the world's population is under 18.

ALL IT TAKES IS A SHEET OF PRINTER PAPER, A FEW FOLDS HERE AND THERE, A LITTLE DEXTERITY, AND MAYBE A LITTLE BREEZE, AND YOU CAN SAIL THIS SIMPLY PERFECT PAPER AIRPLANE UP, UP, AND AWAY. MASTER THIS BASIC DESIGN, AND SEE IF YOU CAN COME UP WITH SOME ALTERNATIVE PLANS. REMEMBER, NEVER MAKE A PAPER AIRPLANE FROM YOUR HOMEWORK, EVEN IF YOU DID GET AN "A" AND WANT THE WHOLE WORLD TO KNOW ABOUT IT.

1 Start with a sheet of printer paper. Fold it along its length to find a center line. Then fold the top two corners down into the center line.

2 Fold those two triangles down. You'll be left with something that looks like an envelope.

3 Fold down the top corners again. The tip of first triangle should stick out.

4 Next, fold the tip up over the triangles to hold them in place.

5 Fold the whole thing in half along the original fold line you found. The small triangle should be on the outside.

6 Fold the wings down. To do this, first bend the paper to find the center line, then crease it along that line.

7 Your paper airplane is ready to launch. **GOOD LUCK!**

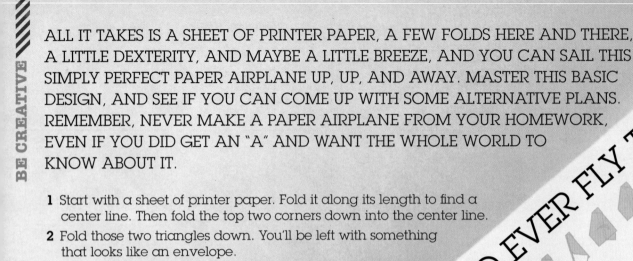

THE BEST PAPER AIRPLANE TO EVER FLY THE SKY

FOLD AN ORIGAMI SWAN

BEHOLD THE BEAUTY OF THE FOLD! LEARN THE ANCIENT ART OF ORIGAMI (PAPER FOLDING) AND YOU CAN TURN A PLAIN OLD SHEET OF PAPER INTO A MINIATURE WORK OF ART. HERE'S HOW TO MAKE A SUPERB SWAN.

1 Start with a square sheet of paper. Fold it down the center to make a triangle, then unfold it so there is a visible crease line.
2 Fold the lower edges of the square into the center crease. You will be left with a shape that looks just like a kite.
3 Now, turn the whole thing over, and make a double fold on each side.
4 Fold the smaller point of the paper upward about halfway along the length to make the swan's neck. Then fold the paper in half lengthwise.
5 Fold the tip down to make the swan's head. Then pull the neck away from the body and slightly unfold the head and body.
6 You could make a whole flock of swans, and turn them into a beautiful mobile to decorate your little brother's room.

HATS OFF TO YOU!

FOLD UP A SHEET OF PAPER INTO A COOL LITTLE HAT. IT ONLY TAKES A MINUTE. WHY NOT MAKE A HAT WITH YOUR HOMEWORK, WEAR IT AROUND A LITTLE, AND SEE IF THE CLOSE CONTACT WITH YOUR BRAIN HELPS YOU TO LEARN STUFF MORE QUICKLY? OR MAKE A NEWSPAPER HAT, AND SEE IF YOU FEEL MORE INFORMED. (IT'S WORTH A TRY...:)

1 Begin with a sheet of printer paper. Put the shorter ends together to fold it in half.
2 Fold in half again to make a crease in the center, then open it out again.
3 Turn down the top corners to meet at the central line.
4 Next, fold one of the long strips up, and fold the triangular tips of the corners over.
5 Finally, fold up the other edge and open your hat.

COVER YOUR ROOM IN SPIDER WEBS

make some super-cool, mega-slimy spider webs to hang in your room. you can make shiny glittery ones, eerie glow-in-the-dark ones, or incredibly creepy, milky white webs. Lay one or two across your journal and you can almost guarantee your little sister will never go near it.

STUFF YOU NEED
marker pen and paper
cardboard
Light-colored plastic bag or garbage bag
Tape
white school glue
Glow-in-the-dark paint or glitter (optional)

WHAT TO DO

1) make a cross on the sheet of paper with a marker, then mark an 'x' on top of the cross. Now, connect the lines to draw a spider web.

2) Put the paper on top of a piece of cardboard. Cut a square from the plastic bag or garbage bag and place it on top of the drawing so the spider web shows through.

3) Open the nozzle of the glue and, holding the bottle close to the plastic, cover over the web with glue. make sure there are no gaps. Leave to dry overnight.

4) when the web is completely dry, carefully peel it off from the plastic backing. For glow-in-the-dark webs, mix a little glowing paint in with the glue. Are these **cool, or what?**

164

HOW TO JUGGLE THREE BEANBAGS

JUGGLING IS A VERY COOL HOBBY. BUT IT'S REALLY TRICKY AT FIRST. WHILE IT MAY SEEM LIKE YOU WILL NEVER GET THE HANG OF JUGGLING, AND YOU SEEM TO SPEND FAR MORE TIME PICKING THE BALLS OFF THE FLOOR THAN WHOOSHING THEM AROUND IN THE AIR, DON'T GIVE UP! ONCE YOU GET THE HANG OF IT, YOU'LL MAKE IT LOOK EASY. (AFTER ALL, YOU CAN JUGGLE YOUR HOMEWORK, YOUR ACTIVITIES, AND YOUR FREE TIME ALREADY, RIGHT?)

Buy (or make) some juggling beanbags to get you started. Bouncy balls do just that—they bounce and roll away when you drop them—and it's just too frustrating.

Get the feel of one beanbag by tossing it up in the air and catching it with one hand. Practice throwing the beanbag from one hand to the other, until it feels natural.

Now pick up a second beanbag. Hold one ball in each hand, and as you toss the ball from your right hand to your left, toss the one in your left hand to the right and catch the one coming across. You'll make mistakes, but you'll learn, promise! Learn to control the bags as you toss them from one hand to the other, with the arc of the bag never going above your eye level.

Ready to try three bags? Hold two bags in your right hand, and the third beanbag in your left hand. Do what you did in Step 3, while holding the third bag. Release the third bag as soon as you catch the second ball in your right hand. Have you got it?

Don't bet your breakfast on it! An egg needs to reach about 160 degrees F. to cook. Even on a sizzling hot day, a sidewalk would rarely reach that temperature, and concrete is a poor conductor of heat, so the egg wouldn't cook evenly. You could probably cook an egg on the hood of a car, though, as metal conducts heat better and gets hotter. (Don't try this without asking an adult first!)

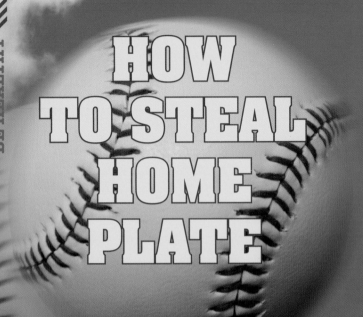

HOW TO STEAL HOME PLATE

So you're standing on third base, with just 90 feet between you and home plate. With two outs, it's time to be a little dangerous out there. The tension builds as the pitcher shoots a wary glance your way, sizing you up. Have you got what it takes to blaze down the third base line and steal home? Do you have the smarts, the speed, and the slide to take you right across the plate? Of course you do. Here's a little bit of coaching. Now, go for it.

1 Take stock. If there are fewer than two outs, it's too risky to try and steal home. Look at the pitcher. Is he distracted? Is he taking a long time to wind up and pitch? Is he throwing lots of breaking balls that take longer to reach the catcher's mitt? Who's at bat? A right-hander may partially shield you from the catcher's view, so he may not see what you're up to and you can take a chance.

2 If the situation fits, take a chance. Yake your lead from third base as the pitcher sets up the pitch, but keep your shoulders facing him. You don't want anyone to see what you're up to until it's too late in the game. When the pitcher lifts his foot and commits to the pitch, get your feet moving. Speed down the line for the plate and run as fast as you can.

3 As you approach the plate, slide like you've never slid before. A hook slide will make it harder for the catcher to tag you out. Hit the dirt, and get your hands or feet on that plate!

Found in the rainforests of Indonesia, the extremely rare Rafflesia arnoldii flower can grow to an amazing 3 feet across, and weigh in at 15 pounds. Here's something even stranger: this freaky flower gives off the smell similar to rotting meat. The foul stench attracts insects that pollinate the plant. You wouldn't want a bouquet of those!

TEN STRANGE AND FASCINATING FACTS ABOUT EVERYBODY'S BODY

(including yours)

There are an incredible 10,000 taste buds on the average tongue, each containing between 30 and 100 taste receptor cells.

THE HUMAN NOSE IS CAPABLE OF DETECTING MORE THAN 10,000 DIFFERENT ODORS.

EACH DAY, YOUR EARS PRODUCE NEW EARWAX THAT PUSHES TINY FLAKES OF OLD EARWAX OUT OF YOUR EARS. YOU CAN'T SEE IT HAPPENING, BUT WHEN YOU TALK, YAWN, OR CHEW, BITS OF OLD EARWAX FALL OUT.

YOUR BRAIN TAKES UP ONLY TWO PERCENT OF YOUR BODY WEIGHT, YET USES 20 PERCENT OF ITS ENERGY.

We lose about 50,000 dead skin cells every minute. If you could collect them (and would you want to?) that's about nine pounds worth of skin flakes a year.

A TAPEWORM IS A RIBBON-LIKE PARASITE THAT MAY LIVE IN THE HUMAN INTESTINES, CLINGING ON TO THE WALLS WITH SUCKERS AND HOOKS. A SINGLE TAPEWORM CAN LIVE FOR MORE THAN 20 YEARS AND GROW TO A DISGUSTING 16 FEET LONG.

THE HUMAN HEART BEATS AN INCREDIBLE 100,800 TIMES A DAY—THAT ADDS UP TO 2.7 BILLION BEATS IN AN AVERAGE LIFETIME—WITHOUT EVER ASKING FOR A DAY OFF.

IN AN AVERAGE LIFETIME, YOU WILL RELEASE AROUND 9,000 GALLONS OF URINE. THAT'S ENOUGH TO FILL UP NEARLY 300 BATHTUBS.

THE HUMAN BODY LOSES ABOUT 0.04 GALLONS OF SWEAT A DAY, EVEN IN COLD WEATHER. BUT IF IT'S A REAL SCORCHER OUTSIDE, YOU CAN SWEAT UP TO 0.2 GALLONS AN HOUR. THE ONLY BODY PARTS WITHOUT SWEAT GLANDS? LIPS AND NIPPLES.

Vomit can be spewed out of your mouth at top speeds of more than 60 miles an hour.

SIT-

SUPERLATIVE

AND POWERFUL

UPS-

Get ready, get set, and get fit! There are more than **650 muscles** in the human body. Why not get off your gluteus maximus (the largest muscle in your body, and yes, it's the one you sit on!) and shape some of them up?

SIT-UPS
This exercise works to tighten the upper abdominal muscles and also helps make your back stronger.

1 Lie on the floor, flat on your back. Bend your knees to a 30-degree angle. You can place your hands behind your neck, or fold your arms across your chest.

2 Now tighten your stomach muscles as hard as you can, and curl your upper body off the floor until you are almost sitting up. Keep your movements smooth. Still keeping the stomach muscles flexed, slowly return to the starting position. Do a set of ten sit-ups, working up to three sets.

CRUNCHES

These work the entire abdominal area and make your lower back stronger. You'll need an exercise bench or a chair.

1 Lie flat on your back on the floor, and put your calves up on the bench or chair. Put your hands behind your neck.

2 Now curl your body upward until your shoulders are off the ground, tightening your stomach muscles as hard as you can. Without releasing your muscles, lower your upper body to the starting position. Do a set of ten crunches, working up to three sets.

PUSH-UPS

This exercise gives a great work out to your upper body— for free!

1 Lie on the floor, chest down, with your hands at shoulder level and palms facing the floor, a little more than shoulder width apart. Your legs should be straight, with feet together and parallel to each other.

2 Keeping your head up and eyes forward, straighten your arms pushing your body off the floor. Keep as straight as you can—try not to arch your back or bend your knees.

3 Phew, did it! Hold for a moment, then slowly return to the starting position.

ESCAPE FROM A SWARM OF BEES

WHILE MOST OF THE TIME BEES JUST BUZZ OFF AND LEAVE YOU ALONE, AT CERTAIN TIMES OF YEAR (SPRING AND FALL) A GROUP OF BEES, FEELING THE SQUEEZE IN THEIR OVERCROWDED COLONY, MIGHT MOVE AWAY IN A MASS CALLED A SWARM TO SET UP A NEW HOME. ONCE THEY BEGIN RAISING BABY BEES IN THE NEWLY ESTABLISHED COLONY, THEY MAY ATTACK TO PROTECT IT. THE BEST WAY TO AVOID A BEE ATTACK IS NOT TO BOTHER A BEE'S COLONY WHEN YOU COME ACROSS ONE. (IF YOU ARE ALLERGIC TO BEES, PLEASE GET AWAY AS FAST AS YOU POSSIBLY CAN.) BUT IF YOU ARE EXTREMELY UNLUCKY, AND THE BEES ATTACK, HERE'S WHAT TO DO.

1 If a swarm of bees starts to gather around you, don't freeze. Get a move on. Don't swat the bees away, as it may make them angry.

2 Get indoors. If there is no shelter, try running through bushes, a cornfield, or some weeds. That will give you a little cover.

3 Don't jump into a lake or a swimming pool. That doesn't even work in cartoons. The bees will probably be there when you get out...and none too happy about the wait.

4 If you do get stung, the bee will leave its stinger in your skin. Try to get it out, so no more of its venom pumps into you. Don't pinch it—that can make matters worse. Instead, try to remove it by pushing your fingernail hard against the stinger, sideways.

HOW TO SHOOT A SLAP SHOT

WHEN YOUR STICK SMACKS against the puck with a resounding slap and shoots off across the ice, you'll know you've nailed a perfect slap shot. This top-notch shot is a tricky one to pull off. It's hard to put a lot of power behind it, yet still aim it accurately, and a blocked slap shot is no fun at all. Still, if you pick your spot, and choose your moment, you can still give the defensive team the jitters with a wicked slap shot. So get your skates on, and here we go.

1 Get into position. Stand with your feet a little wider than shoulder width apart, with the puck centered between your skates and far enough out so you can eyeball the puck when you look straight down.

2 Keep your top hand in the normal place on the stick, but slide your bottom hand down the handle about six inches. This will help put some power behind your shot. Hold on to that stick firmly, and keep your eyes on the puck.

3 Draw your stick back to about waist height. Your weight should be on your back leg. Now bring the stick down toward the puck. As you swing, transfer your weight from your back skate to your front. Lean into the shot as with your entire body.

4 Your stick should hit the ice just behind the puck first. Keep gripping with your bottom hand. Snap your wrists as the stick strikes the puck, sending it off with maximum power, and follow through the shot, pointing the stick blade at the target. Whammy!

Unfortunately not. By the time you are seven years old, your brain is about 95 percent of its adult size. Sorry. But you should still do your homework.

SLAM IT, JAM IT, THROW IT DOWN, and rattle that rim. Is there anything cooler than pulling off a perfect slam-dunk shot? Sure, you get the same two points for a slam-dunk as you do for any other basket, but it feels so right to slam that b-ball right through the hoop. If you are tall enough to jump and nearly touch the rim, you should be ready to learn how to slam-dunk. So, if you've got it, here's how to jump it and slam it.

1 Dribble up to the basket at high speed. Move with confidence and be aggressive. Approach the basket in the same way you do for a lay-up shot, keeping your eyes on the square just above the rim.

2 Pick up the ball when you are about 10 to 12 feet from the basket. Continue to move to your goal, taking your allowed two steps as you grip the ball firmly in both hands. (You need really big hands to be able to palm a basketball, so unless that's you, stick with a two-handed grip.)

3 Push up from your second step to the rim, jumping as high as you possibly can. Stretch your arms toward the basket, aiming just above the rim. Ready?

4 Jam the ball down right through the rim! Land on both feet, and wait for the crowd to go wild. Be cool, though—you want it to look as if you slam-dunk all the time. No biggie, right?

HOW TO SLAM-DUNK
A BASKETBALL

HOW TO CATCH A HAIL MARY PASS

AS THE CLOCK RUNS DOWN, time is literally running out for your football team. There is no time for strategy. The only thing that can give you a shot at winning the game is pure instinct and a sheer miracle. The quarterback, under pressure from the defense, sends his pass soaring in a desperation play. The spiraling pigskin arcs through the sky straight toward...you. Will you catch the miracle pass and save the game? Yes, you will. Here's how.

1 Focus your eyes on the ball once it is airborne. If you take your concentration off that ball, even for a moment, you can miss the catch. Ignore the rest of the world. It's just you and the football.

2 Here it comes. Stay calm and keep your focus. Extend your arms and hands. Make a triangle with your hands, palms facing away from the body. Point your thumbs at each other and all your other fingers up.

3 You want the tip of the football to head through the triangle. When it's about halfway through your hands, clamp down on it with your fingers.

4 Now get that ball secure, tucking it into your chest Don't make your move until it is firmly in your possession.

5 Go, go, go! Get yourself into the end zone. You can work miracles.

TEN
MIND-BOGGLING
TRANSPORTATION
FACTS

ALTHOUGH THE LONDON **UNDERGROUND** SUBWAY SYSTEM IS THE WORLD'S OLDEST (IT OPENED IN 1863), THE NEW YORK MTA SYSTEM HAS THE MOST STOPS, WITH **468 STATIONS**.

THE FASTEST **JET** ON RECORD IS THE US MILITARY'S TWO-SEAT BLACKBIRD. IN 1964, IT FLEW AT **MACH 3.0**—THAT'S THREE TIMES THE SPEED OF SOUND.

The longest single train ride in the world is on the **Trans-Siberian Railway**. This epic journey from Moscow, Russia to Pyongyang, North Korea spans **6,346 miles** and takes **eight** days.

The longest freight train in history rolled out from the BHP mining company in Australia, in 2001. The train's **682** carriages spanned a total of some **4.6 miles**.

THE LONGEST TRAFFIC JAM IN THE WORLD STRETCHED FROM LYONS, FRANCE TO THE FRENCH CAPITAL

IN JULY 2000, 18 PEOPLE SQUEEZED THEMSELVES INTO A MINI COOPER IN BIRMINGHAM, ENGLAND, SETTING A NEW RECORD FOR THE MOST MINI PASSENGERS.

The best-selling car in the world is the **Toyota Corolla**. Since the first one rolled off the assembly line in 1966, more than **66 million** Corollas have been built across the globe.

HARTSFIELD-JACKSON AIRPORT, ATLANTA, GEORGIA IS THE WORLD'S BUSIEST PASSENGER AIRPORT. IN A TYPICAL YEAR, THE AIRPORT HANDLES 86,000,000 PEOPLE.

DUTCH CYCLIST FRED ROMPELBERG REACHED THE FASTEST RECORDED BICYCLE SPEED AT BONNEVILLE FLATS, UTAH IN 1995. HIS BEST TIME WAS AN ASTONISHING 166.9 MILES AN HOUR.

The busiest railway system in the world is the **East Japan Railway Company**, serving the city of Tokyo as well as eastern Japan. More than **16 million** passengers use the service every day.

PARIS ON 16 FEBRUARY, 1980. THE TRAFFIC WAS BUMPER-TO-BUMPER FOR **109 MILES**.

HOW TO SCORE A PENALTY KICK

IN A SOCCER PENALTY KICK, it's just you against the goalkeeper, one-on-one. Maybe one team has committed a foul within its own penalty area. Maybe teams are still tied after two overtimes, and the penalty shootout decides the victor. Whatever the reason you are standing out there, just a dozen yards in front of the net, it can feel like the scariest place on the planet. Don't let the pressure get to you. Be confident, be cool, take a deep breath, and kick that ball right on home.

1 Relax and have faith in your abilities. OK, you are alone out there, but your team is behind you. Try to block everything out and focus on the job at hand.

2 Plan your move. Decide where you're going to put the ball. Aiming for a high or low corner on either side of the net is a pretty good bet, but make your decision based on your own strengths.

3 Focus. As you make your move, don't waver. Stay steady and strong. Keep your eyes on the ball and your target area.

4 The goalkeeper will be doing what he or she can to distract you—don't let it happen. Move on in and get the job done. **GOAL!**

Oh, yes. Spirit and Opportunity, a pair of robots launched by NASA, landed on Mars in 2004. They were built for a three-month mission but the incredible machines have already crisscrossed the Red Planet for four years!

SHOW YOUR RESPECT FOR THE STARS AND STRIPES

WE SEE THE UNITED STATES FLAG FLYING JUST ABOUT EVERYWHERE WE GO...OUTSIDE SCHOOL, UP AND DOWN THE STREETS OF THE TOWN, AND IN AND AROUND THE NEIGHBORHOOD. THE STARS AND STRIPES IS ONE OF THE MOST IMPORTANT SYMBOLS OF OUR COUNTRY. IF YOU STOP AND THINK FOR A MOMENT ABOUT ALL THE THINGS THE AMERICAN FLAG REPRESENTS—THE HISTORY AND THE FUTURE OF OUR COUNTRY, ALL THE PEOPLE WHO LIVE IN IT, AND THE MANY DIFFERENT WAYS WE ARE FREE TO LIVE—YOU'LL ALSO UNDERSTAND HOW IMPORTANT IT IS TO TREAT THE FLAG WITH RESPECT.

RAISING AND LOWERING THE STARS AND STRIPES

You need a team of two to raise and lower the flag. One person holds the folded flag (remember, our flag must never touch the ground) while the other person attaches it to the halyard (flag line). He or she pulls the line tight to raise the flag swiftly. After the flag lifts away from the flag carrier's arms and is flying at the top of the staff, the carrier should salute it as his or her partner ties the halyard securely.

To lower the flag, one person unties the halyard and pulls on the line to slowly lower the flag, while his or her partner salutes. As the flag nears the ground, the saluting partner gathers it in his arms to keep it off the ground, and the other person detaches the flag and ties up the lines.

FOLDING THE FLAG

Treating the flag with respect at all times includes folding it correctly. You will need a partner to help you. First, fold the flag in half along its length, and then again in half lengthwise. Keep the starry blue field on the outside. Next, the person at the other end of the blue field makes a triangular fold at the end of the flag and continues to fold it up, one triangle at a time, until nothing shows but a triangle of blue. Tuck the strip that attaches the flag into the fold to make a neat package.

LONG MAY SHE WAVE

The American flag can fly with pride every day of the year, but it is especially important to raise it on national holidays. The flag is usually raised from sunrise to sunset, at full-staff (that means it is all the way to the top of the flagpole.) To mark the death of an important public figure, or honor those who have given their lives for their country, the flag is flown at half-staff (a distance halfway between the top and bottom of the pole.)

HOW TO DISPLAY OLD GLORY

When displayed with other flags, the US flag should fly higher than the others, or should extend out farther. In a row of flags, Old Glory should be farthest to its own right. If you are carrying the flag in a parade, hold it up and aloft on its staff.

THE PLEDGE OF ALLEGIANCE

I PLEDGE ALLEGIANCE TO THE FLAG
OF THE UNITED STATES OF AMERICA.
AND TO THE REPUBLIC, FOR WHICH IT STANDS,
ONE NATION, UNDER GOD, INDIVISIBLE,
WITH LIBERTY AND JUSTICE FOR ALL.

COOL AREA
↓
www.kiddk.com/handbook

Tag, you're it!

GRAB YOUR FRIENDS, hit the park or backyard, and play a classic game of tag. The rules are simple: everyone runs around and whoever is "It" tries to touch someone on the shoulder, who then becomes "It" and so on. Kids have played this game for centuries, for one good reason: it's good fun! The more people you can round up, the better. So, go on, get outside and play.

It's a jungle out there. Well, not really, but there are some plants you need to steer clear of when you are traipsing around the great outdoors. Plants such as poison ivy, poison oak, and poison sumac contain an oily sap in their leaves, stems, and even roots. If this sticky goo comes into contact with your skin, you can develop a really nasty, itchy rash. The best way to avoid these pesky plants is to learn how to spot them, and then stay away. (It's also a good idea to wear long pants in areas where these plants are found.) Here's a guide to a toxic trio of plants.

HOW TO AVOID ITCHY, SCRATCHY POISONOUS PLANTS

Poison ivy: watch out for leaves grouped in threes. Poison ivy grows at the edges of woods and fields, or in sunny spots. It may grow as a bush or climbing vine. Its leaves are bright green in spring, turning darker in fall.

Poison oak: these also have leaves grouped in threes, but they are ruffled at the edges. The plant thrives in scrubby patches and in the woods. Its leaves are usually bright green in spring, changing color to red or orange in the fall.

Poison sumac: this plant grows in swampy wet areas as a shrub or small-ish tree. It has long stems tipped with six to a dozen smallish leaves arranged in pairs, a little like a feather. Its seed pods are found between the leaves and the branches (in non-poisonous sumac, the pods are at the end of the branches.)

What to do in case of contact: the sap has to sit on your skin for 10 minutes or so before it starts to irritate you, so if you wash off the sap right away with soap and water, you may prevent a rash. If you can, change your clothes, as the sap can stay on them. If you are unlucky, calamine lotion applied to the rash can usually stop the worst of the itching.

PSSST!
It's me again.

If you're reading this, you are very near to the end of the book. **(UNLESS YOU'RE SKIPPING AHEAD—AND WHY DO THAT? DON'T YOU LIKE SURPRISE ENDINGS?)** Anyway, I guess this would be a good place for the big finish, the grand finale, the final bow—that kind of thing. **YEP?** NOPE.

There can't be an ending, because when you **KICK-START YOUR IMAGINATION**, light up your brain, and get your get-up-and-go going, there's no stopping you. So use this book as a starting point to help you think up all kinds of other stuff to do. **SHARE IT WITH YOUR FRIENDS AND PUT YOUR HEADS TOGETHER.** You'll never have nothing to do, ever again.

AND THAT'S OFFICIALLY OFFICIAL.

INDEX

A

aardvarks 96
airplanes 12–13, 162, 178
airports 179
aliens 112–13
allegiance, pledge of 183
allergies 51
alligators 98–9
ambulances 51
animals 96–7
   arthropods 60–61
   bears 30–31, 86–7
   big cats 40–41
   dinosaurs 39, 57
   fish 80–81
   jokes 26
   pets 152–3
   tracking 48–9, 100–101
anteaters, giant 97
ants on a log 70
arachnids 60
arm-wrestling 54
arthropods 60–61
artwork, sidewalk chalk 56
Assassin 75
Atlanta airport 179
autumn leaves 107
avalanches 114–15
avocados 71

B

backpacks 145
balloons, water 54
bandannas 136
bank accounts 35
baseball 166, 177
basketball 176
beaches 104–5
beanbags, juggling 164
bears 30–31, 86–7, 96
bedrooms, cleaning 22–3
bees, swarm of 172–3
beetles 61, 128–9
bicycles 50, 79, 179
big cats 40–41
birds 46–7
   chicken 39, 57
   evolution 57
   flamingoes 96
   feeding 134
   owl pellets 101
   swifts 97
boats 105
bones 126–7
boots, hiking 110
brains 140, 168, 175
bubble-blowing contest 76–7
bugs 44–5, 61, 109, 143
burgers 156
buses, safety 50
butterflies 60–61, 128–9

C

caimans 98
camels 97
campfires 141
camping trips 144–9, 150–51
can openers 65
carbon monoxide detectors 51
card games 150
cars 165, 179
catching snakes 120
cats 40–41, 152
centipedes 60, 143
chalk, sidewalk 56
cheesy dip 71
chicken 39, 57
chocolate 157
cleaning
   bedrooms 22–3
   bicycles 79
climbing trees 24
clothes 73, 111
clouds 138–9
clues, treasure hunt 58–9
cockroaches 128, 129
code, Morse 38
computer viruses 36
cooking 70–71, 146–7
coolers 146–7
crabs 61
crocodiles 98
crunches 171
crustaceans 61
crystals 122–3

D

deer droppings 100, 101
deluxe popcorn toppers 70
diaries 104
dinosaurs 39, 57
dips 71
dogs 96, 152
dreams 42, 121

droppings, animals 100–101
duck droppings 100
Durand, Peter 65

E

e-mail 36
ears, frogs 117, 149
earthquakes 51
earthworms 90–91
earwax 168
eggs, frying 108, 165
entomology 128–9
evolution, birds 57
exercises 170–71
eyes, and sneezing 142, 154

F

families 130–31
fireflies 62–3
fires 51, 141
first-aid kit 51
fish 80–81
   pets 153
   sharks 118–19
flag 182–3
flamingos 96
flashlight tag 38
flashlights 145
flies 61, 96, 128
flowers, largest 158, 167
flying disks 38
food
   bear safety 86–7
   camping trips 147
   cookouts 156–7

INDEX

snacks 70–71
fox droppings 101
freezer fruit 70
freight trains 178
friends 18–19
frogs 117, 149
fruit, freezer 70

G

games 151
    Assassin 75
    Hostage 43
    Manhunt! 75
    marbles 16
    paper, rock, scissors 154
    tag 38, 184
    treasure hunt 58–9
garbage 85
glass, sea 104
good deeds 116
graphite 135
grass, playing a blade of 154
guacamole 71
guinea pigs 153

H

Hail Mary passes 177
hamburger heaven 156
hammocks 88–9
hamsters 153
hand shadow puppets 32, 150
hats, paper 163
heart beats 169
hello 124
herbivores 100
herpetology 68–9
hiking 110–11
    guidelines 137

meeting bears 30–31
    walking sticks 109
history, local 66–7
home safety 51
homework 17, 140, 175
Hostage 43
hot-diggety dogs 156
houseflies 96, 128
hurricanes 51
hyraxes 96

I

ice hockey 174
ichthyology 80–81
igloos 34
insects 60–61, 128–9
    bites and stings 51
    bug traps 143
    fireflies 62–3
Internet 36–7

J

Japanese railways 179
jeans 73
jet planes 178
jokes 26–9, 150
journals 104
juggling 164
jump ropes 106

K

keyhole trick 93
kindness 116
knock-knock jokes 28, 150

L

landfills 85

languages 124
leaves, autumn 107
lemonade stands 78
libraries 66
lizards 153
local history 66–7
London Underground 178

M

Manhunt! 75
marbles 16
Mars 160, 181
marshmallows 157
matches 147
meteoroids 33, 55
millipedes 60
Mini Coopers 179
money 35
Morse Code 38
moths 97
mountain lions 40–41
mountains 114–15
muscles 170–71
museums 67

N

Neolithic noodles 125
New York MTA system 178
noodles 125
nose
    sense of smell 168
    writing with 93
nuked quesadillas 70
numbers 161

O

origami swan 163
ornithology 46–7

otter droppings 100
owl pellets 101

P

paper
    airplanes 162
    hats 163
    origami swan 163
    tricks 92, 93
paper, rock, scissors 154
parasites 169
passwords 37
pasta 94, 125
pellets, owl 101
penalty kicks 180
pencils 74, 135
pets 152–3
pit toilets 148
pizzas in the oven 71
planet, saving 82–3
plants, poisonous 184–5
pledge of allegiance 183
poisons
    plants 184–5
    poison control centers 51
    snakes 97
polar bears 96
police 51
Polo, Marco 125
popcorn toppers 70
pots and pans 146
puppets, shadow 32, 150
push-ups 171

Q

quesadillas, nuked 70

R

rabbit droppings 100, 101
rabbits 153
Rafflesia 167
railways 178, 179
rats 21, 72, 101
recycling 73, 83, 84–5
reptiles 68–9
robots 160, 181
rock hyraxes 96
rockpool viewer 105
roe deer 100
Rompelberg, Fred 179
ropes
    jump ropes 106
    tug of war 32

S

safety 50–53
    alligators 98
    avalanches 114–15
    bears 30–31, 86–7
    campfires 141
    home safety 51
    mountain lions 40–41
    poisonous plants 184–5
    school safety 50
    sharks 118–19
    swarms of bees 172–3
    travel 50
sand sculpture 105
saving money 35
scarecrows 20
scat 100–101
school jokes 27
school safety 50
scorpions 60
sculpture 34, 105

sea glass 104
seashells 104
seashore 104–5
shadow puppets 32, 150
sharks 118–19
shells 104
shoes, hiking 110
showers, portable 148
sidewalks
    frying eggs on 108, 165
    sidewalk chalk 56
sisters, being nice to 88
sit-ups 170
skeleton 126–7
skin cells 169
slam-dunk shots 176
slap shots 174
sleeping bags 145
slime 89
smell, sense of 168
smiling 88
smoke detectors 51
smoothies 70
s'mores 157
snacks 70–71
snakes 68–9
    catching 120
    pets 153
    safety 14–15
    venom 97
sneezing 142, 154
snow 34
    avalanches 114–15
    snowball fights 64
soap bubble-blowing contest 76–7
soccer 180
social networking sites 37
socks, hiking 111
spaghetti 94
spider webs 164

spiders 60
squid, giant 97
Stars and Stripes 182–3
story-telling 150
stoves, camp 146
subways 178
swan, origami 163
swarms of bees 172–3
sweat 21, 72, 96, 169
swifts 97

T

tag 38, 184
taipan snakes 97
tapeworms 169
tarps 145
taste buds 168
tents 145
thumb-wrestling 54
tin cans 25, 65
toilets, pit 148
tongue-twisters 102–3
tongues 168
tornadoes 51
tortoises 153
town history 66–7
Toyota Corolla 179
tracking animals 48–9, 100–101
traffic jams 178–9
trail mix 71
trains 178, 179
Trans-Siberian Railway 178
transportation 178–9
trash 85
travel, safety 50
treasure hunt 58–9
trees
    adopting 43
    age 133

climbing 24
    height 132–3
tricks 92–3, 136
tug of war 32
Tyrannosaurus rex 39, 57

U

urine 169

V

venom, snakes 97
very berry smoothie 70
viruses, computer 36
volunteer projects 95
vomit 169

W

walking safety 50
walking sticks 109
washing, on camping trips 148
water balloons 54
webs, spider 164
websites 36
wigwams 159
wild cat droppings 101
willow wigwams 159
worm farms 90–91
writing with your nose 93

XYZ

Picture Credits

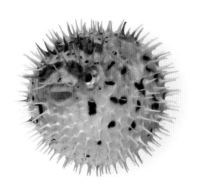